TRIPPING...

You don't really need grass ... Put enough writing talent and enough imagination and enough discipline (it's that last one that is rare) together and you have a combination that can blow your mind any day of the week. And a few days that aren't in any week ...

Especially if it's science fiction

Especially good science fiction

Especially Robert Silverberg

THE REALITY TRIP

And Other Implausibilities

Robert Silverberg

BALLANTINE BOOKS • NEW YORK
An Intext Publisher

SBN 345-02548-2-095

First Printing: March, 1972

Printed in Canada

BALLANTINE BOOKS, INC.
101 Fifth Avenue, New York, N.Y. 10003

Contents

The Reality Trip

And Other Implausibilities

In Entropy's Jaws

Static crackles from the hazy golden cloud of air-borne loudspeakers drifting just below the ceiling of the spaceliner cabin. A hiss: communications filters are opening. An impending announcement from the bridge, no doubt. Then the captain's bland, mechanical voice: "We are approaching the Panama Canal. All passengers into their bottles until the all-clear after insertion. When we come out the far side, we'll be traveling at eighty lights toward the Perseus relay booster. Thank you." In John Skein's cabin the warning globe begins to flash, dousing him with red, yellow, green light, going up and down the visible spectrum, giving him some infra- and ultra- too. Not everybody who books passage on this liner necessarily has human sensory equipment. The signal will not go out until Skein is safely in his bottle. Go on, it tells him. Get in. Get in. Panama Canal coming up.

Obediently he rises and moves across the narrow cabin toward the tapering dull-skinned steel container, two and a half meters high, that will protect him against the dimensional stresses of canal insertion. He is a tall, angular man with thin lips, a strong chin, glossy black hair that clings close to his high-vaulted skull. His skin is deeply tanned but his eyes are those of one who has been in winter for some time. This is the fiftieth year of his second go-round. He is traveling alone toward a world of the Abbondanza system, perhaps the last leg on a journey that has occupied him for several years.

The passenger bottle swings open on its gaudy rhodium-jacketed hinge when its sensors, picking up Skein's mass and thermal output, tell it that its protectee is within entry range. He gets in. It closes and seals, wrapping him in a seamless magnetic field. "Please be seated," the bottle tells him softly. "Place your arms through the stasis loops and your feet in the security platens. When you have done this the pressor fields will automatically be activated and you will be fully insulated against injury during the coming period of turbulence." Skein, who has had plenty of experience with faster-than-light travel, has anticipated the instructions and is already in stasis. The bottle closes. "Do you wish music?" it asks him. "A book? A vision spool? Conversation?"

"Nothing, thanks," Skein says, and waits.

He understands waiting very well by this time. Once he was an impatient man, but this is a thin season in his life, and it has been teaching him the arts of stoic acceptance. He will sit here with the Buddha's own complacency until the ship is through the canal. Silent, alone, self-sufficient. If only there will be no fugues this time. Or, at least—he is negotiating the terms of his torment with his demons—at least let there be no flashforwards. If he must break loose again from the matrix of time, he prefers to be cast only into his yesterdays, never into his tomorrows.

"We are almost into the canal now," the bottle tells him pleasantly.

"It's all right. You don't need to look after me. Just let me know when it's safe to come out."

He closes his eyes. Trying to envision the ship: a fragile glimmering purple needle squirting through clinging blackness, plunging toward the celestial vortex just ahead, the maelstrom of clashing forces, the soup of contravariant tensors. The Panama Canal, so-called. Through which the liner will shortly rush, acquiring during its passage such a garland of borrowed power that it will rip itself free of the standard fourspace; it will emerge on the far side of the canal into a strange, tranquil pocket of the universe where the speed of light is the downside limiting velocity, and no one knows where the upper limit lies.

Alarms sound in the corridor, heavy, resonant: clang, clang, clang. The dislocation is beginning. Skein is braced. What does it look like out there? Folds of glowing black velvet, furry swatches of the disrupted continuum, wrapping themselves around the ship? Titanic lightnings hammering on the hull? Laughing centaurs flashing across the twisted heavens? Despondent masks, fixed in tragic grimaces, dangling between the blurred stars? Streaks of orange, green, crimson: sick rainbows, limp, askew? In we go. *Clang, clang, clang.* The next phase of the voyage now begins. He thinks of his destination, holding an image of it rigidly in mind. The picture is vivid, though this is a world he has visited only in spells of temporal fugue. Too often; he has been there again and again in these moments of disorientation in time. The colors are wrong on that world. Purple sand. Blue-leaved trees. Too much manganese? Too little copper? He will forgive it its colors if it will grant him his answers. And then. Skein feels the familiar ugly throbbing at the base of his neck, as if the tip of his spine is swelling like a balloon. He curses. He tries to resist. As he feared, not even the bottle can wholly protect him against these stresses. Outside the ship the universe is being wrenched apart; some of that slips in here and throws him into a private epilepsy of the time-line. Space-time is breaking up for him. He will go into fugue. He clings, fighting, knowing it is futile. The currents of time buffet him, knocking him a short distance into the future, then a reciprocal distance into the past, as if he is a bubble of insect spittle glued loosely to a dry reed. He cannot hold on much longer. Let it not be flashforward, he prays, wondering who it is to whom he prays. Let it not be flash-forward. And he loses his grip. And shatters. And is swept in shards across time.

Of course, if x *is before* y *then it remains eternally before* y, *and nothing in the passage of time can change this. But the peculiar position of the "now" can be easily expressed simply because our language has tenses. The future* will be, *the present* is, *and the past* was; *the light will be red, it is now yellow, and it was green. But do we, in these terms, really describe the "processional" character of time? We sometimes say that an event is future, then it is present, and finally it is past; and by this means we seem to dispense with tenses, yet we portray the passage of time. But this is really not the case; for all that we have done is to translate our tenses into the words "then" and "finally," and into the order in which we state our clauses. If we were to omit these words or their equivalents, and mix up the clauses, our sentences would no longer be meaningful. To say that the future, the present, and the past* are *in some sense* is *to dodge the problem of time by resorting to the tense-less language of logic and mathematics. In such an* atemporal *language it would be meaningful to say that Socrates is mortal because all men are mortal and Socrates is a man, even though Socrates has been dead many centuries. But if we cannot describe time either by a language containing tenses or by a tenseless language, how* shall *we symbolize it?*

He feels the curious doubleness of self, the sense of having been here before, and knows it is flashback. Some comfort in that. He is a passenger in his own skull, looking out through the eyes of John Skein on an event that he has already experienced, and which he now is powerless to alter.

His office. All its gilded magnificence. A crystal dome at the summit of Kenyatta Tower. With the amplifiers on he can see as far as Serengeti in one direction, Mombasa in another. Count the fleas on an elephant in Tsavo Park. A wall of light on the east-southeast face of the dome, housing his data-access units. No one can stare at that wall more than thirty seconds without suffering intensely from a surfeit of information. Except Skein; he drains nourishment from it, hour after hour.

As he slides into the soul of that earlier Skein he takes a brief joy in the sight of his office, like Aeneas relishing a vision of unfallen Troy, like Adam looking back into Eden. How good it was. That broad sweet desk with its subtle components dedicated to his service. The gentle psychosensitive carpet, so useful and so beautiful. The undulating ribbon-sculpture gliding in and out of the dome's skin, undergoing molecular displacement each time and forever exhibiting the newest of its infinity of possible patterns. A rich man's office; he was unabashed in his pursuit of elegance. He had earned the right to luxury through the intelligent use of his innate skills. Returning now to that lost dome of wonders, he quickly seizes his moment of satisfaction, aware that shortly some souring scene of subtraction will be replayed for him, one of the stages in the darkening and withering of his life. But which one?

"Send in Coustakis," he hears himself say, and his words give him the answer. That one. He will again watch his own destruction. Surely there is no further need to subject him to this particular re-enactment. He has been through it at least seven times; he is losing count. An endless spiraling track of torment.

Coustakis is bald, blue-eyed, sharp-nosed, with the desperate look of a man who is near the end of his first go-round and is not yet sure that he will be granted a second. Skein guesses that he is about seventy. The man is unlikable: he dresses coarsely, moves in aggressive blurting little strides, and shows in every gesture and glance that he seethes with envy of the opulence with which Skein surrounds himself. Skein feels no need to like his clients, though. Only to respect. And Coustakis is brilliant; he commands respect.

Skein says, "My staff and I have studied your proposal in great detail. It's a cunning scheme."

"You'll help me?"

"There are risks for me," Skein points out. "Nissenson has a powerful ego. So do you. I could get hurt. The whole concept of synergy involves risk for the Communicator. My fees are calculated accordingly."

"Nobody expects a Communicator to be cheap," Coustakis mutters.

"I'm not. But I think you'll be able to afford me. The question is whether I can afford you."

"You're very cryptic, Mr. Skein. Like all oracles."

Skein smiles. "I'm not an oracle, I'm afraid. Merely a conduit through whom connections are made. I can't foresee the future."

"You can evaluate probabilities."

"Only concerning my own welfare. And I'm capable of arriving at an incorrect evaluation."

Coustakis fidgets. "Will you help me or won't you?"

"The fee," Skein says, "is half a million down, plus an equity position of fifteen percent in the corporation you'll establish with the contacts I provide."

Coustakis gnaws at his lower lip. "So much?"

"Bear in mind that I've got to split my fee with Nissenson. Consultants like him aren't cheap."

"Even so. Ten percent."

"Excuse me, Mr. Coustakis. I really thought we were past the point of negotiation in this transaction. It's going to be a busy day for me, and so—" Skein passes his hand over a black rectangle on his desk and a section of the floor silently opens, uncovering the dropshaft access. He nods toward it. The carpet reveals the colors of Coustakis' mental processes: black for anger, green for greed, red for anxiety, yellow for fear, blue for temptation, all mixed together in the hashed pattern betraying the calculations now going on in his mind. Coustakis will yield. Nevertheless Skein proceeds with the charade of standing, gesturing toward the exit, trying to usher his visitor out. "All right," Coustakis says explosively, "fifteen percent!"

Skein instructs his desk to extrude a contract cube. He says, "Place your hand here, please," and as Coustakis touches the cube he presses his own palm against its opposite face. At once the cube's sleek crystalline surface darkens and roughens as the double sensory output bombards it. Skein says, "Repeat after me. I, Nicholas Coustakis, whose handprint and vibration pattern are being imprinted in this contract as I speak—"

"I, Nicholas Coustakis, whose handprint and vibration pattern are being imprinted in this contract as I speak—"

"—do knowingly and willingly assign to John Skein Enterprises, as payment for professional services to be rendered, an equity interest in Coustakis Transport Ltd. or any successor corporation amounting to—"

"—do knowingly and willingly assign—"

They drone on in turns through a description of Coustakis' corportaion and the irrevocable nature of Skein's part ownership in it. Then Skein files the contract cube and says, "If you'll phone your bank and put your thumb on the cash part of the transaction, I'll make contact with Nissenson and you can get started."

"Half a million?"

"Half a million."

"You know I don't have that kind of money."

"Let's not waste time, Mr. Coustakis. You have assets. Pledge them as collateral. Credit is easily obtained."

Scowling, Coustakis applies for the loan, gets it, transfers the funds to Skein's account. The process takes eight minutes; Skein uses the time to review Coustakis' ego profile. It displeases Skein to have to exert such sordid economic pressures; but the service he offers does, after all, expose him to dangers, and he must cushion the risk by high guarantees, in case some mishap should put him out of business.

"Now we can proceed," Skein says, when the transaction is done.

Coustakis has almost invented a system for the economical instantaneous transportation of matter. It will not, unfortunately, ever be useful for living things, since the process involves the destruction of the material being shipped and its virtually simultaneous reconstitution elsewhere. The fragile entity that is the soul cannot withstand the withering blast of Coustakis' transmitter's electron beam. But there is tremendous potential in the freight business; the Coustakis transmitter will be able to send cabbages to Mars, computers to Pluto, and, given the proper linkage facilities, it should be able to reach the inhabited extrasolar planets.

However, Coustakis has not yet perfected his system. For five years he has been stymied by one impassable problem: keeping the beam tight enough between transmitter and receiver. Beam-spread has led to chaos in his experiments; marginal straying results in the loss of transmitted information, so that that which is being sent invariably arrives incomplete. Coustakis has depleted his resources in the unsuccessful search for a solution, and thus has been forced to the desperate and costly step of calling in a Communicator.

For a price, Skein will place him in contact with someone who can solve his problem. Skein has a network of consultants on several worlds, experts in technology and finance and philology and nearly everything else. Using his own mind as the focal nexus, Skein will open telepathic communion between Coustakis and a consultant.

"Get Nissenson into a receptive state," he orders his desk.

Coustakis, blinking rapidly, obviously uneasy, says, "First let me get it clear. This man will see everything that's in my mind? He'll get access to my secrets?"

"No. No. I filter the communion with great care. Nothing will pass from your mind to his except the nature

of the problem you want him to tackle. Nothing will
come back from his mind to yours except the answer."

"And if he doesn't have the answer?"

"He will."

Skein gives no refunds in the event of failure, but he
has never had a failure. He does not accept jobs that he
feels will be inherently impossible to handle. Either Nissenson will see the solution Coustakis has been overlooking, or else he will make some suggestion that will
nudge Coustakis toward finding the solution himself. The
telepathic communion is the vital element. Mere talking
would never get anywhere. Coustakis and Nissenson could
stare at blueprints together for months, pound computers
side by side for years, debate the difficulty with each other
for decades, and still they might not hit on the answer.
But the communion creates a synergy of minds that is
more than a doubling of the available brainpower. A
union of perceptions, a heightening, that always produces
that mystic flash of insight, that leap of the intellect.

"And if he goes into the transmission business for himself afterward?" Coustakis asks.

"He's bonded," Skein says curtly. "No chance of it.
Let's go, now. Up and together."

The desk reports that Nissenson, half the world away
in São Paulo, is ready. Skein's power does not vary with
distance. Quickly he throws Coustakis into the receptive
condition, and swings around to face the brilliant lights
of his data-access units. Those sparkling, shifting little
blazes kindle his gift, jabbing at the electrical rhythms of
his brain until he is lifted into the energy level that permits
the opening of a communion. As he starts to go up, the
other Skein who is watching, the time-displaced prisoner
behind his forehead, tries frenziedly to prevent him from
entering the fatal linkage. *Don't. Don't. You'll overload.
They're too strong for you.* Easier to halt a planet in its
orbit, though. The course of the past is frozen; all this
has already happened; the Skein who cries out in silent

anguish is merely an observer, necessarily passive, here to view the maiming of his earlier self.

Skein reaches forth one tendril of his mind and engages Nissenson. With another tendril he snares Coustakis. Steadily, now, he draws the two tendrils together.

There is no way to predict the intensity of the forces that will shortly course through his brain. He has done what he could, checking the ego profiles of his client and the consultant, but that really tells him little. What Coustakis and Nissenson may be as individuals hardly matters; it is what they may become in communion that he must fear. Synergic intensities are unpredictable. He has lived for a lifetime and a half with the possibility of a burnout.

The tendrils meet.

Skein the observer winces and tries to armor himself against the shock. But there is no way to deflect it. Out of Coustakis' mind flows a description of the matter transmitter and a clear statement of the beam-spread problem; Skein shoves it along to Nissenson, who begins to work on a solution. But when their minds join it is immediately evident that their combined strength will be more than Skein can control. This time the synergy will destroy him. But he cannot disengage; he has no mental circuitbreaker. He is caught, trapped, impaled. The entity that is Coustakis/Nissenson will not let go of him, for that would mean its own destruction. A wave of mental energy goes rippling and dancing along the vector of communion from Coustakis to Nissenson and goes bouncing back, pulsating and gaining strength, from Nissenson to Coustakis. A fiery oscillation is set up. Skein sees what is happening; he has become the amplifier of his own doom. The torrent of energy continues to gather power each time it reverberates from Coustakis to Nissenson, from Nissenson to Coustakis. Powerless, Skein watches the energy-pumping effect building up a mighty charge. The discharge is bound to come soon, and he will be the one who must receive it. How long? How long? The juggernaut fills the corridors of his mind. He ceases to know which end of the circuit is Nissenson, which is Coustakis; he perceives only two shining walls of mental power, between which he is stretched ever thinner, a twanging wire of ego, heating up, heating up, glowing now, emitting a searing blast of heat, particles of identity streaming away from him like so many liberated ions—

Then he lies numb and dazed on the floor of his office, grinding his face into the psychosensitive carpet, while Coustakis barks over and over, "Skein? Skein? Skein? Skein?"

Like any other chronometric device, our inner clocks are subject to their own peculiar disorders and, in spite of the substantial concordance between private and public time, discrepancies may occur as the result of sheer inattention. Mach noted that if a doctor focuses his attention on the patient's blood, it may seem to him to squirt out before the lancet enters the skin and, for similar reasons, the feebler of two stimuli presented simultaneously is usually perceived later. . . . Normal life requires the capacity to recall experiences in a sequence corresponding, roughly at least, to the order in which they actually occurred. It requires in addition that our potential recollections should be reasonably accessible to consciousness. These potential recollections mean not only a perpetuation within us of representations of the past, but also a ceaseless interplay between such representations and the uninterrupted input of present information from the external world. Just as our past may be at the service of our present, so the present may be remotely controlled by our past: in the words of Shelley, "Swift as a Thought by the snake Memory stung."

"Skein? Skein? Skein? Skein?"

His bottle is open and they are helping him out. His cabin is full of intruders. Skein recognizes the captain's robot, the medic, and a couple of passengers, the little swarthy man from Pingalore and the woman from Globe Fifteen. The cabin door is open and more people are coming in. The medic makes a cuff-shooting gesture and a blinding haze of metallic white particles wraps itself about Skein's head. The little tingling prickling sensations spur him to wakefulness. "You didn't respond when the bottle told you it was all right," the medic explains. "We're through the canal."

"Was it a good passage? Fine. Fine. I must have dozed."

"If you'd like to come to the infirmary—a routine check, only—put you through the diagnostat—"

"No. No. Will you all please go? I assure you, I'm quite all right."

Reluctantly, clucking over him, they finally leave. Skein gulps cold water until his head is clear. He plants himself flatfooted in midcabin, trying to pick up some sensation of forward motion. The ship now is traveling at something like fifteen million miles a second. How long is fifteen million miles? How long is a second? From Rome to Naples it was a morning's drive on the autostrada. From Tel Aviv to Jerusalem was the time between twilight and darkness. San Francisco to San Diego spanned lunch to dinner by superpod. As I slide my right foot two inches forward we traverse fifteen million miles. From where to where? And why? He has not seen Earth in twenty-six months. At the end of this voyage his remaining funds will be exhausted. Perhaps he will have to make his home in the Abbondanza system; he has no return ticket. But of course he can travel to his heart's discontent within his own skull, whipping from point to point along the time-line in the grip of the fugues.

He goes quickly from his cabin to the recreation lounge.

The ship is a second-class vessel, neither lavish nor seedy. It carries about twenty passengers, most of them, like him, bound outward on one-way journeys. He has not talked directly to any of them, but he has done considerable eavesdropping in the lounge, and by now can tag each one of them with the proper dull biography.

The wife bravely joining her pioneer husband, whom she has not seen for half a decade. The remittance man under orders to place ten thousand light-years, at the very least, between himself and his parents. The glittery-eyed entrepreneur, a Phoenician merchant sixty centuries after his proper era, off to carve an empire as a middleman's middleman. The tourists. The bureaucrat. The colonel. Among this collection Skein stands out in sharp relief; he is the only one who has not made an effort to know and be known, and the mystery of his reserve tantalizes them.

He carries the fact of his crackup with him like some wrinkled dangling yellowed wen. When his eyes meet those of any of the others he says silently, You see my deformity? I am my own survivor. I have been destroyed and lived to look back on it. Once I was a man of wealth and power, and look at me now. But I ask for no pity. Is that understood?

Hunching at the bar, Skein pushes the node for filtered rum. His drink arrives, and with it comes the remittance man, handsome, young, insinuating. Giving Skein a confidential wink, as if to say, *I* know. You're on the run, too.

"From Earth, are you?" he says to Skein.

"Formerly."

"I'm Pid Rocklin."

"John Skein."

"What were you doing there?"

"On Earth?" Skein shrugs. "A Communicator. I retired four years ago."

"Oh." Rocklin summons a drink. "That's good work, if you have the gift."

"I had the gift," Skein says. The unstressed past tense is as far into self-pity as he will go. He drinks and pushes for another one. A great gleaming screen over the bar shows the look of space: empty, here beyond the Panama Canal, although yesterday a million suns blazed on that ebony rectangle. Skein imagines he can hear the whoosh of hydrogen molecules scraping past the hull at eighty lights. He sees them as blobs of brightness millions of miles long, going *zip!* and *zip!* and *zip!* as the ship spurts along. Abruptly a purple nimbus envelops him and he drops into a flashforward fugue so quickly there is not even time for the usual futile resistance. "Hey, what's the matter?" Pid Rocklin says, reaching for him. "Are you all—" and Skein loses the universe.

He is on the world that he takes to be Abbondanza VI, and his familiar companion, the skull-faced man, stands beside him at the edge of an oily orange sea. They appear to be having the debate about time once again. The skull-faced man must be at least a hundred twenty years old; his skin lies against his bones with, seemingly, no flesh at all under it, and his face is all nostrils and burning eyes. Bony sockets, sharp shelves for cheekbones, a bald dome of a skull. The neck no more than wrist-thick, rising out of shriveled shoulders. Saying, "Won't you ever come to see that causality is merely an illusion, Skein? The notion that there's a consecutive series of events is nothing but a fraud. We impose form on our lives, we talk of time's arrow, we say that there's a flow from A through G and Q to Z, we make believe everything is nicely linear. But it isn't, Skein. It isn't."

"So you keep telling me."

"I feel an obligation to awaken your mind to the truth. G can come before A, and Z before both of them. Most of us don't like to perceive it that way, so we arrange things in what seems like a more logical pattern, just as a novelist will put the motive before the murder and the murder before the arrest. But the universe isn't a novel. We can't make nature imitate art. It's all random, Skein, random, random! Look there. You see what's drifting on the sea?"

On the orange waves tosses the bloated corpse of a shaggy blue beast. Upturned saucery eyes, drooping snout, thick limbs. Why is it not waterlogged by now? What keeps it afloat?

The skull-faced man says, "Time is an ocean, and events come drifting to us as randomly as dead animals on the waves. We filter them. We screen out what doesn't make sense and admit them to our consciousness in what seems to be the right sequence." He laughs. "The grand delusion! The past is nothing but a series of films slipping unpredictably into the future. And vice versa."

"I won't accept that," Skein says stubbornly. "It's a demonic, chaotic, nihilistic theory. It's idiocy. Are we graybeards before we're children? Do we die before we're born? Do trees devolve into seeds? Deny linearity all you like. I won't go along."

"You can say that after all you've experienced?"

Skein shakes his head. "I'll go on saying it. What I've been going through is a mental illness. Maybe I'm deranged, but the universe isn't."

"Contrary. You've only recently become sane and started to see things as they really are," the skull-faced man insists. "The trouble is that you don't want to admit the evidence you've begun to perceive. Your filters are down, Skein! You've shaken free of the illusion of linearity! Now's your chance to show your resilience. Learn to live with the real reality. Stop this silly business of imposing an artificial order on the flow of time. Why *should* effect follow cause? Why *shouldn't* the seed follow the tree? Why must you persist in holding tight to a useless, outworn, contemptible system of false evaluations of experience when you've managed to break free of the—"

"Stop it! Stop it! Stop it! Stop it!"

"—right, Skein?"

"What happened?"

"You started to fall off your stool," Pid Rocklin says. "You turned absolutely white. I thought you were having some kind of a stroke."

"How long was I unconscious?"

"Oh, three, four seconds, I suppose. I grabbed you and propped you up, and your eyes opened. Can I help you to your cabin? Or maybe you ought to go to the infirmary."

"Excuse me," Skein says hoarsely, and leaves the lounge.

When the hallucinations began, not long after the Coustakis overload, he assumed at first that they were memory disturbances produced by the fearful jolt he had absorbed. Quite clearly most of them invoked scenes of his past, which he would relive, during the moments of fugue, with an intensity so brilliant that he felt he had actually been thrust back into time. He did not merely recollect, but rather he experienced the past anew, following a script from which he could not deviate as he spoke and felt and reacted. Such strange excursions into memory could be easily enough explained: his brain had been damaged, and it was heaving old segments of experience into view in some kind of attempt to clear itself of debris and heal the wounds. But while the flashbacks were comprehensible, the flashforwards were not, and he did not recognize them at all for what they actually were. Those scenes of himself wandering alien worlds, those phantom conversations with people he had never met, those views of spaceliner cabins and transit booths and unfamiliar hotels and passenger terminals, seemed merely to be fantasies, random fictions of his injured brain. Even when he started to notice that there was a consistent pattern to these feverish glimpses of the unknown, he still did not catch on. It appeared as though he was seeing himself performing a sort of quest, or perhaps a pilgrimage; the slices of unexperienced experience that he was permitted to see began to fit into a coherent structure of travel and seeking. And certain scenes and conversations recurred, yes, sometimes several times the same day, the script always the same, so that he began to learn a few of the scenes word for word. Despite the solid texture of these episodes, he persisted in thinking of them as mere brief flickering segments of nightmare. He could not imagine why the injury to his brain was causing him to have these waking dreams of long space voyages and unknown planets, so vivid and so momentarily real, but they seemed no more frightening to him than the equally vivid flashbacks.

Only after a while, when many months had passed since the Coustakis incident, did the truth strike him. One day he found himself living through an episode that he considered to be one of his fantasies. It was a minor thing, one that he had experienced, in whole or in part, seven or eight times. What he had seen, in fitful bursts of un-invited delusion, was himself in a public garden on some hot spring morning, standing before an immense baroque building while a grotesque group of non-human tourists filed past him in a weird creaking, clanking procession of inhalator suits and breather-wheels and ion-disperser masks. That was all. Then it happened that a harrowing legal snarl brought him to a city in North Carolina about fourteen months after the overload, and, after having put in his appearance at the courthouse, he set out on a long walk through the grimy, decayed metropolis, and came, as if by an enchantment, to a huge metal gate behind which he could see a dark sweep of lavish forest, oaks and rhododendrons and magnolias, laid out in an elegant formal manner. It was, according to a sign posted by the gate, the estate of a nineteenth-century millionaire, now open to all and preserved in its ancient state despite the encroachments of the city on its borders. Skein bought a ticket and went in, on foot, hiking for what seemed like miles through cool leafy glades, until abruptly the path curved and he emerged into the bright sunlight and saw before him the great gray bulk of a colossal mansion, hundreds of rooms topped by parapets and spires, with a massive portico from which vast columns of stairs descended. In wonder he moved toward it, for this was the building of his frequent fantasy, and as he approached he beheld the red and green and purple figures crossing the portico, those coiled and gnarled and looping shapes he had seen before, the eerie horde of alien travelers here to take in the wonders of Earth. Heads without eyes, eyes without heads, multiplicities of limbs and absences of limbs, bodies like tumors and tumors like bodies, all the universe's imagination on display in these agglomerated life-forms, so strange and yet not at all strange to him. But this time it was no fantasy. It fit smoothly into the sequence of the events of the day, rather than dropping, dreamlike, intrusive, into that sequence. Nor did it fade after a few moments; the scene remained sharp, never leaving him to plunge back into "real" life. This was reality itself, and he had experienced it before.

Twice more in the next few weeks things like that happened to him, until at last he was ready to admit the truth to himself about his fugues, that he was experiencing flashforwards as well as flashbacks, that he was being subjected to glimpses of his own future.

T'ang, the high king of the Shang, asked Hsia Chi saying, "In the beginning, were there already individual things?" Hsia Chi replied, "If there were no things then, how could there be any now? If later generations should pretend that there had been no things in our time, would they be right?" T'ang said, "Have things then no before and no after?" To which Hsia Chi replied, "The ends and the origins of things have no limit from which they began. The origin of one thing may be considered the end of another; the end of one may be considered the origin of the next. Who can distinguish accurately between these cycles? What lies beyond all things, and before all events, we cannot know."

They reach and enter the Perseus relay booster, which is a whirling celestial anomaly structurally similar to the Panama Canal but not nearly so potent, and it kicks the ship's velocity to just above a hundred lights. That is the voyage's final acceleration; the ship will maintain this rate for two and a half days, until it clocks in at Scylla, the main deceleration station for this part of the galaxy, where it will be seized by a spongy web of forces twenty light-minutes in diameter and slowed to sublight velocities for the entry into the Abbondanza system.

Skein spends nearly all of this period in his cabin, rarely eating and sleeping very little. He reads almost constantly, obsessively dredging from the ship's extensive library a wide and capricious assortment of books. Rilke. Kafka. Eddington, *The Nature of the Physical World*. Lowry, *Hear Us O Lord From Heaven Thy Dwelling Place*. Elias. Razhuminin. Dickey. Pound. Fraisse, *The Psychology of Time*. Greene, *Dream and Delusion*. Poe. Shakespeare. Marlowe. Tourneur. *The Waste Land*. *Ulysses*. *Heart of Darkness*. Bury, *The Idea of Progress*. Jung. Büchner. Pirandello. *The Magic Mountain*. Ellis, *The Rack*. Cervantes. Blenheim. Fierst. Keats. Nietzsche. His mind swims with images and bits of verse, with floating sequences of dialogue, with unscaffolded dialectics. He dips into each work briefly, magpielike, seeking bright scraps. The words form a scaly impasto on the inner surface of his skull. He finds that this heavy verbal overdose helps, to some slight extent, to fight off the fugues; his mind is weighted, perhaps, bound by this leaden clutter of borrowed genius to the moving line of the present, and during his debauch of reading he finds himself shifting off that line less frequently than in the recent past. His mind whirls. *Man is a rope stretched between the animal and the Superman—A rope over an abyss.* My patience are exhausted. *See, see where Christ's blood streams in the firmament! One drop would save my soul.* I had not thought death had undone so many. These fragments I have shored against my ruins. *Hoogspanning. Levensgevaar. Peligro de Muerte. Electricidad. Danger.* Give me my spear. *Old father, old artificer, stand me now and ever in good stead.* You like this garden? Why is it yours? We evict those who destroy! *And then went down to the ship, set keel to breakers, forth on the godly sea.* There is no "official" theory of time, defined in creeds or universally agreed upon among

Christians. Christianity is not concerned with the purely scientific aspects of the subject nor, within wide limits, with its philosophical analysis, except insofar as it is committed to a fundamentally realist view and could not admit, as some Eastern philosophies have done, that temporal existence is mere illusion. *A shudder in the loins engenders there the broken wall, the burning roof and tower and Agamemnon dead.* Stately, plump Buck Mulligan came from the stairhead, bearing a bowl of lather on which a mirror and a razor lay crossed. *In what distant deeps or skies burnt the fire of thine eyes? On what wings dare he aspire? What the hand dare seize the fire?* These fragments I have shored against my ruins. Hieronymo's mad againe. *Then felt I like some watcher of the skies when a new planet swims into his ken.* It has also lately been postulated that the physical concept of information is identical with a phenomenon of reversal of entropy. The psychologist must add a few remarks here: It does not seem convincing to me that information is *eo ipso* identical with a *pouvoir d'organisation* which undoes entropy. *Datta. Dayadhvam. Damyata. Shantih shantih shantih*

Nevertheless, once the ship is past Scylla and slowing toward the Abbondanza planets, the periods of fugue become frequent once again, so that he lives entrapped, shuttling between the flashing shadows of yesterday and tomorrow.

After the Coustakis overload he tried to go on in the old way, as best he could. He gave Coustakis a refund without even being asked, for he had been of no service, nor could he ever be. Instantaneous transportation of matter would have to wait. But Skein took other clients. He could still make the communion, after a fashion, and when the nature of the task was sufficiently low-level he could even deliver a decent synergetic response.

Often his work was unsatisfactory, however. Contacts would break at awkward moments, or, conversely, his

filter mechanism would weaken and he would allow the
entire contents of his client's mind to flow into that
of his consultant. The results of such disasters were chaotic, involving him in heavy medical expenses and sometimes in damage suits. He was forced to place his fees
on a contingency basis: no synergy, no pay. About half
the time he earned nothing for his output of energy.
Meanwhile his overhead remained the same as always:
the domed office, the network of consultants, the research staff, and the rest. His effort to remain in business was eating rapidly into the bank accounts he had
set aside against just such a time of storm.

They could find no organic injury to his brain. Of
course, so little was known about a Communicator's gift
that it was impossible to determine much by medical
analysis. If they could not locate the center from which
a Communicator powered his communions, how could
they detect the place where he had been hurt? The medical archives were of no value; there had been eleven
previous cases of overload, but each instance was phys-
iologically unique. They told him he would eventually
heal, and sent him away. Sometimes the doctors gave him
silly therapies: counting exercises, rhythmic blinkings, hop-
ping on his left leg and then his right, as if he had had a
stroke. But he had not had a stroke.

For a time he was able to maintain his business on
the momentum of his reputation. Then, as word got
around that he had been hurt and was no longer any
good, clients stopped coming. Even the contingency basis
for fees failed to attract them. Within six months he
found that he was lucky to find a client a week. He re-
duced his rates, and that seemed only to make things
worse, so he raised them to something not far below
what they had been at the time of the overload. For a
while the pace of business increased, as if people were
getting the impression that Skein had recovered. He gave
such spotty service, though. Blurred and wavering com-

munions, unanticipated positive feedbacks, filtering problems, information deficiencies, redundancy surpluses—
"You take your mind in your hands when you go to Skein," they were saying now.

The fugues added to his professional difficulties.

He never knew when he would snap into hallucination. It might happen during a communion, and often did. Once he dropped back to the moment of the Coustakis-Nissenson hookup and treated a terrified client to a replay of his overload. Once, although he did not understand at the time what was happening, he underwent a flashforward and carried the client with him to a scarlet jungle on a formaldehyde world, and when Skein slipped back to reality the client remained in the scarlet jungle. There was a damage suit over that one, too.

Temporal dislocation plagued him into making poor guesses. He took on clients whom he could not possibly serve, and wasted his time on them. He turned away people whom he might have been able to help to his own profit. Since he was no longer anchored firmly to his timeline, but drifted in random oscillations of twenty years or more in either direction, he forfeited the keen sense of perspective on which he had previously founded his professional judgments. He grew haggard and lean, also. He passed through a tempest of spiritual doubts that amounted to total submission and then total rejection of faith within the course of four months. He changed lawyers almost weekly. He liquidated assets with invariably catastrophic timing to pay his cascading bills.

A year and a half after the overload, he formally renounced his registration and closed his office. It took six months more to settle the remaining damage suits. Then, with what was left of his money, he bought a space-liner ticket and set out to search for a world with purple sand and blue-leaved trees, where, unless his fugues had played him false, he might be able to arrange for the repair of his broken mind.

Now the ship has returned to the conventional four-space and dawdles planetward at something rather less than half the speed of light. Across the screens there spreads a necklace of stars; space is crowded here. The captain will point out Abbondanza to anyone who asks: a lemon-colored sun, bigger than that of Earth, surrounded by a dozen bright planetary pips. The passengers are excited. They buzz, twitter, speculate, anticipate. No one is silent except Skein. He is aware of many love affairs; he has had to reject several offers just in the past three days. He has given up reading and is trying to purge his mind of all he has stuffed into it. The fugues have grown worse. He has to write notes to himself, saying things like *You are a passenger aboard a ship heading for Abbondanza VI, and will be landing in a few days,* so that he does not forget which of his three entangled time-lines is the true one.

Suddenly he is with Nilla on the island in the Gulf of Mexico, getting aboard the little excursion boat. Time stands still here; it could almost be the twentieth century. The frayed, sagging cords of the rigging. The lumpy engine inefficiently converted from internal combustion to turbines. The mustachioed Mexican bandits who will be their guides today. Nilla, nervously coiling her long blonde hair, saying, "Will I get seasick, John? The boat rides right in the water, doesn't it? It won't even hover a little bit?"

"Terribly archaic," Skein says. "That's why we're here."

The captain gestures them aboard. Juan, Francisco, Sebastián. Brothers. *Los hermanos.* Yards of white teeth glistening below the drooping mustaches. With a terrible roar the boat moves away from the dock. Soon the little town of crumbling pastel buildings is out of sight and they are heading jaggedly eastward along the coast, green shoreward water on their left, the blue depths on the right. The morning sun coming up hard. "Could I sunbathe?" Nilla asks. Unsure of herself; he has never seen her this way, so hesitant, so abashed. Mexico has robbed her of her New York assurance. "Go ahead," Skein says. "Why not?" She drops her robe. Underneath she wears only a waist-strap; her heavy breasts look white and vulnerable in the tropic glare, and the small nipples are a faded pink. Skein sprays her with protective sealant and she sprawls out on the deck. *Los hermanos* stare hungrily and talk to each other in low rumbling tones. Not Spanish. Mayan, perhaps? The natives have never learned to adopt the tourists' casual nudity here. Nilla, obviously still uneasy, rolls over and lies face down. Her broad smooth back glistens.

Juan and Francisco yell. Skein follows their pointing fingers. Porpoises! A dozen of them, frisking around the bow, keeping just ahead of the boat, leaping high and slicing down into the blue water. Nilla gives a little cry of joy and rushes to the side to get a closer look. Throwing her arm self-consciously across her bare breasts. "You don't need to do that," Skein murmurs. She keeps herself covered. "How lovely they are," she says softly. Sebastián comes up beside them. *"Amigos,"* he says. "They are. My friends." The cavorting porpoises eventually disappear. The boat bucks bouncily onward, keeping close to the island's beautiful empty palmy shore. Later they anchor, and he and Nilla swim masked, spying on the coral gardens. When they haul themselves on deck again it is almost noon. The sun is terrible. "Lunch?" Francisco asks. "We make you good lunch now?" Nilla laughs. She is no longer hiding her body. "I'm starved!" she cries.

"We make you good lunch," Francisco says, grinning, and he and Juan go over the side. In the shallow water they are clearly visible near the white sand of the bottom. They have spear-guns; they hold their breaths and prowl. Too late Skein realizes what they are doing. Francisco hauls a fluttering spiny lobster out from behind a rock. Juan impales a huge pale crab. He grabs three conchs also, surfaces, dumps his prey on the deck.

Francisco arrives with the lobster. Juan, below again, spears a second lobster. The animals are not dead; they crawl sadly in circles on the deck as they dry. Appalled, Skein turns to Sebastián and says, "Tell them to stop. We're not that hungry." Sebastián, preparing some kind of salad, smiles and shrugs. Francisco has brought up another crab, bigger than the first. "Enough," Skein says. *"Basta! Basta!"* Juan, dripping, tosses down three more conchs. "You pay us good," he says. "We give you good lunch." Skein shakes his head. The deck is becoming a slaughterhouse for ocean life. Sebastián now energetically splits conch shells, extracts the meat, drops it into a vast bowl to marinate in a yellow-green fluid. *"Basta!"* Skein yells. Is that the right word in Spanish? He knows it's right in Italian. *Los hermanos* look amused. The sea is full of life, they seem to be telling him. We give you good lunch. Suddenly Francisco erupts from the water, bearing something immense. A turtle! Forty, fifty pounds! The joke has gone too far. "No," Skein says. "Listen, I have to forbid this. Those turtles are almost extinct. Do you understand that? *Muerto. Perdido. Desaparecido.* I won't eat a turtle. Throw it back. Throw it back." Francisco smiles. He shakes his head. Deftly he binds the turtle's flippers with rope. Juan says, "Not for lunch, *señor.* For us. For to sell. *Mucho dinero."* Skein can do nothing. Francisco and Sebastián have begun to hack up the crabs and lobsters. Juan slices peppers into the bowl where the conchs are marinating. Pieces of dead animals litter the deck. "Oh, I'm *starving,"* Nilla says. Her waiststrap is off too, now. The turtle watches the whole scene, beady-eyed. Skein shudders. Auschwitz, he thinks. Buchenwald. For the animals it's Buchenwald every day.

Purple sand, blue-leaved trees. An orange sea gleaming not far to the west under a lemon sun. "It isn't much farther," the skull-faced man says. "You can make it. Step by step by step is how."

"I'm winded," Skein says. "Those hills—"

"I'm twice your age, and I'm doing fine."

"You're in better shape. I've been cooped up on space-ships for months and months."

"Just a short way on," says the skull-faced man. "About a hundred meters from the shore."

Skein struggles on. The heat is frightful. He has trouble getting a footing in the shifting sand. Twice he trips over black vines whose fleshly runners form a mat a few centimeters under the surface; loops of the vines stick up here and there. He even suffers a brief fugue, a seven-second flashback to a day in Jerusalem. Somewhere at the core of his mind he is amused by that: a flashback within a flashforward. Encapsulated concentric hallucina-tions. When he comes out of it, he finds himself getting to his feet and brushing sand from his clothing. Ten steps onward the skull-faced man halts him and says, "There it is. Look there, in the pit."

Skein sees a funnel-shaped crater right in front of him, perhaps five meters in diameter at ground level and dwindling to about half that width at its bottom, some six or seven meters down. The pit strikes him as a series of perfect circles making up a truncated cone. Its sides are smooth and firm, almost glazed, and the sand has a brown tinge. In the pit, resting peacefully on the flat floor, is something that looks like a golden amoeba the size of a large cat. A row of round blue-black eyes crosses the hump of its back. From the perimeter of its body comes a soft green radiance.

"Go down to it," the skull-faced man says. "The force of its power falls off with the cube of the distance; from up here you can't feel it. Go down. Let it take you over. Fuse with it. Make communion, Skein, make com-munion!"

"And will it heal me? So that I'll function as I did before the trouble started?"

"If you let it heal you, it will. That's what it wants to do. It's a completely benign organism. It thrives on repairing broken souls. Let it into your head; let it find the damaged place. You can trust it. Go down."

Skein trembles on the edge of the pit. The creature below flows and eddies, becoming first long and narrow, then high and squat, then resuming its basically circular form. Its color deepens almost to scarlet, and its radiance shifts toward yellow. As if preening and stretching itself. It seems to be waiting for him. It seems eager. This is what he has sought so long, going from planet to wearying planet. The skull-faced man, the purple sand, the pit, the creature. Skein slips his sandals off. *What have I to lose?* He sits for a moment on the pit's rim; then he shimmies down, sliding part of the way, and lands softly, close beside the being that awaits him. And immediately feels its power.

He enters the huge desolate cavern that is the cathedral of Haghia Sophia. A few Turkish guides lounge hopefully against the vast marble pillars. Tourists shuffle about, reading to each other from cheap plastic guidebooks. A shaft of light enters from some improbable aperture and splinters against the Moslem pulpit. It seems to Skein that he hears the tolling of bells and feels incense prickling at his nostrils. But how can that be? No Christian rites have been performed here in a thousand years. A Turk looms before him. "Show you the mosyics?" he says. *Mosyics.* "Help you understand this marvelous building? A dollar. No? Maybe change money? A good rate. Dollars, marks, Eurocredits, what? You speak English? Show you the mosyics?" The Turk fades. The bells grow louder. A row of bowed priests in white silk robes files past the altar, chanting in—what? Greek? The ceiling is encrusted with gems. Gold plate gleams everywhere. Skein senses the terrible complexity of the cathedral, teeming now with life, a whole universe engulfed in this gloom, a thousand chapels packed with worshippers, long lines waiting to urinate in the crypts, a marketplace in the balcony, jeweled necklaces changing hands with low murmurs of negotiation, babies being born behind the alabaster sarcophagi, the bells tolling, dukes nodding to one another, clouds of incense swirling toward the dome, the figures in the mosaics alive, making the sign of the Cross, smiling, blowing kisses, the pillars moving now, becoming fat-middled as they bend from side to side, the entire colossal structure shifting and flowing and melting. And a ballet of Turks. "Show you the mosyics?" "Change money?" "Postcards? Souvenir of Istanbul?" A plump, pink American face: "You're John Skein, aren't you? The Communicator? We worked together on the big fusion-chamber merger in '53." Skein shakes his head. "It must be that you are mistaken," he says, speaking in Italian. "I am not he. Pardon. Pardon." And joins the line of chanting priests.

Purple sand, blue-leaved trees. An orange sea under a lemon sun. Looking out from the top deck of the terminal, an hour after landing, Skein sees a row of towering hotels rising along the nearby beach. At once he feels the wrongness: there should be no hotels. The right planet has no such towers; therefore this is another of the wrong ones.

He suffers from complete disorientation as he attempts to place himself in sequence. *Where am I?* Aboard a liner heading toward Abbondanza VI. *What do I see?* A world I have previously visited. *Which one?* The one with the hotels. The third out of seven, isn't it?

He has seen this planet before, in flashforwards. Long before he left Earth to begin his quest he glimpsed those hotels, that beach. Now he views it in flashback. That perplexes him. He must try to see himself as a moving point traveling through time, viewing the scenery now from this perspective, now from that.

He watches his earlier self at the terminal. Once it was his future self. How confusing, how needlessly muddling! "I'm looking for an old Earthman," he says. "He must be a hundred, hundred twenty years old. A face like a skull—no flesh at all, really. A brittle man. No? Well, can you tell me, does this planet have a life-form about this big, a kind of blob of golden jelly, that lives in pits down by the seashore, and—No? No? Ask someone else, you say? Of course. And perhaps a hotel room? As long as I've come all this way."

He is getting tired of finding the wrong planets. What folly this is, squandering his last savings on a quest for a world seen in a dream! He would have expected planets with purple sand and blue-leaved trees to be uncommon, but no, in an infinite universe one can find a dozen of everything, and now he has wasted almost half his money and close to a year, visiting two planets and this one and not finding what he seeks.

He goes to the hotel they arrange for him.

The beach is packed with sunbathers, most of them from Earth. Skein walks among them. "Look," he wants to say, "I have this trouble with my brain, an old injury, and it gives me these visions of myself in the past and future, and one of the visions I see is a place where there's a skull-faced man who takes me to a kind of amoeba in a pit that can heal me, do you follow? And it's a planet with purple sand and blue-leaved trees, just like this one, and I figure if I keep going long enough I'm bound to find it and the skull-face and the amoeba, do you follow me? And maybe this is the planet after all, only I'm in the wrong part of it. What should I do? What hope do you think I really have?" This is the third world. He knows that he must visit a number of wrong ones before he finds the right one. But how many? How many? And when will he know that he has the right one?

Standing silent on the beach, he feels confusion come over him, and drops into fugue, and is hurled to another world. Purple sand, blue-leaved trees. A fat, friendly Pingalorian consul. "A skull-faced man? No, I can't say I know of any." Which world is this, Skein wonders? One that I have already visited, or one that I have not yet come to? The manifold layers of illusion dazzle him. Past and future and present lie like a knot around his throat. Shifting planes of reality; intersecting films of event. Purple sand, blue-leaved trees. Which planet is this? Which one? Which one? He is back on the crowded beach. A lemon sun. An orange sea. He is back in his cabin on the spaceliner. He sees a note in his own handwriting: *You are a passenger aboard a ship heading for Abbondanza VI, and will be landing in a few days.* So everything was a vision. Flashback? Flashforward? He is no longer able to tell. He is baffled by these identical worlds. Purple sand. Blue-leaved trees. He wishes he knew how to cry.

Instead of a client and a consultant for today's communion, Skein has a client and a client. A man and a woman, Michaels and Miss Schumpeter. The communion is of an unusually intimate kind. Michaels has been married six times, and several of the marriages apparently have been dissolved under bitter circumstances. Miss Schumpeter, a woman of some wealth, loves Michaels but doesn't entirely trust him; she wants a peep into his mind before she'll put her thumb to the marital cube. Skein will oblige. The fee has already been credited to his account. Let me not to the marriage of true minds admit impediments. If she does not like what she finds in her beloved's soul, there may not be any marriage, but Skein will have been paid.

A tendril of his mind goes to Michaels, now. A tendril to Miss Schumpeter. Skein opens his filters. "Now you'll meet for the first time," he tells them. Michaels flows to her. Miss Schumpeter flows to him. Skein is merely the conduit. Through him pass the ambitions, betrayals, failures, vanities, deteriorations, disputes, treacheries, lusts, generosities, shames, and follies of these two human beings. If he wishes, he can examine the most private sins of Miss Schumpeter and the darkest yearnings of her future husband. But he does not care. He sees such things every day. He takes no pleasure in spying on the psyches of these two. Would a surgeon grow excited over the sight of Miss Schumpeter's Fallopian tubes or Michaels' pancreas? Skein is merely doing his job. He is no voyeur, simply a Communicator. He looks upon himself as a public utility.

When he severs the contact, Miss Schumpeter and Michaels both are weeping.

"I love you!" she wails.

"Get away from me!" he mutters.

Purple sand. Blue-leaved trees. Oily orange sea.

The skull-faced man says, "Won't you ever come to see that causality is merely an illusion, Skein? The notion that there's a consecutive series of events is nothing but a fraud. We impose form on our lives, we talk of time's arrow, we say that there's a flow from A through G and Q to Z, we make believe everything is nicely linear. But it isn't, Skein. It isn't."

"So you keep telling me."

"I feel an obligation to awaken your mind to the truth. G can come before A, and Z before both of them. Most of us don't like to perceive it that way, so we arrange things in what seems like a more logical pattern, just as a novelist will put the motive before the murder and the murder before the arrest. But the universe isn't a novel. We can't make nature imitate art. It's all random, Skein, random, random!"

"Half a million?"

"Half a million."

"You know I don't have that kind of money."

"Let's not waste time, Mr. Coustakis. You have assets. Pledge them as collateral. Credit is easily obtained." Skein waits for the inventor to clear his loan. "Now we can proceed," he says, and tells his desk, "Get Nissenson into a receptive state."

Coustakis says, "First let me get it clear. This man

will see everything that's in my mind? He'll get access to my secrets?"

"No. No. I filter the communion with great care. Nothing will pass from your mind to his except the nature of the problem you want him to tackle. Nothing will come back from his mind to yours except the answer."

"And if he doesn't have the answer?"

"He will."

"And if he goes into the transmission business for himself afterward?"

"He's bonded," Skein says curtly. "No chance of it. Let's go, now. Up and together."

"Skein? Skein? Skein? Skein?"

The wind is rising. The sand, blown aloft, stains the sky gray. Skein clambers from the pit and lies by its rim, breathing hard. The skull-faced man helps him get up.

Skein has seen this series of images hundreds of times.

"How do you feel?" the skull-faced man asks.

"Strange. Good. My head seems so clear!"

"You had communion down there?"

"Oh, yes. Yes."

"And?"

"I think I'm healed," Skein says in wonder. "My strength is back. Before, you know, I felt cut down to the bone, a minimum version of myself. And now. And now." He lets a tendril of consciousness slip forth. It meets the mind of the skull-faced man. Skein is aware of a glassy interface; he can touch the other mind, but he cannot enter it. "Are you a Communicator too?" Skein asks, awed.

"In a sense. I feel you touching me. You're better, aren't you?"

"Much. Much. Much."

"As I told you. Now you have your second chance, Skein. Your gift has been restored. Courtesy of our friend in the pit. They love being helpful."

"Skein? Skein? Skein? Skein?"

We conceive of time either as flowing or as enduring. The problem is how to reconcile these concepts. From a purely formalistic point of view there exists no difficulty, as these properties can be reconciled by means of the concept of a duratio successiva. *Every unit of time measure has this characteristic of a flowing permanence: an hour streams by while it lasts and so long as it lasts. Its flowing is thus identical with its duration. Time, from this point of view, is transitory;* but its passing away lasts.

In the early months of his affliction he experienced a great many scenes of flashforward while in fugue. He saw himself outside the nineteenth-century mansion, he saw himself in a dozen lawyers' offices, he saw himself in hotels, terminals, spaceliners, he saw himself discussing the nature of time with the skull-faced man, he saw himself trembling on the edge of the pit, he saw himself emerging healed, he saw himself wandering from world to world, looking for the right one with purple sand and blue-leaved trees. As time unfolded most of these flashforwards duly entered the flow of the present; he *did* come to the mansion, he *did* go to those hotels and terminals, he *did* wander those useless worlds. Now, as he approaches Abbondanza VI, he goes through a great many flashbacks and a relatively few flashforwards, and the flashforwards seem to be limited to a fairly narrow span of time, covering his landing on Abbondanza VI, his first meeting with the skull-faced man, his journey to the pit, and his emergence, healed, from the amoeba's lair. Never anything beyond that final scene. He wonders if time is going to run out for him on Abbondanza VI.

The ship lands on Abbondanza VI half a day ahead of schedule. There are the usual decontamination procedures to endure, and while they are going on Skein rests in his cabin, counting minutes to liberty. He is curiously confident that this will be the world on which he finds the skull-faced man and the benign amoeba. Of course, he has felt that way before, looking out from other space-liners at other planets of the proper coloration, and he has been wrong. But the intensity of his confidence is something new. He is sure that the end of his quest lies here.

"Debarkation beginning now," the loudspeakers say.

He joins the line of outgoing passengers. The others smile, embrace, whisper; they have found friends or even mates on this voyage. He remains apart. No one says goodbye to him. He emerges into a brightly lit terminal, a great cube of glass that looks like all the other ter-minals scattered across the thousands of worlds that man has reached. He could be in Chicago or Johannesburg or Beirut: the scene is one of porters, reservations clerks, customs officials, hotel agents, taxi drivers, guides. A blight of sameness spreading across the universe. Stum-bling through the customs gate, Skein finds himself set upon. Does he want a taxi, a hotel room, a woman, a man, a guide, a homestead plot, a servant, a ticket to Abbondanza VII, a private car, an interpreter, a bank, a telephone? The hubbub jolts Skein into three consecu-tive ten-second fugues, all flashbacks; he sees a rainy day in Tierra del Fuego, he conducts a communion to help a maker of sky-spectacles perfect the plot of his latest extravaganza, and he puts his palm to a cube in order to dictate contract terms to Nicholas Coustakis. Then Coustakis fades, the terminal reappears, and Skein realizes that someone has seized him by the left arm just above the elbow. Bony fingers dig painfully into his flesh. It is the skull-faced man. "Come with me," he says. "I'll take you where you want to go."

"This isn't just another flashforward, is it?" Skein asks, as he has watched himself ask so many times in the past. "I mean, you're really here to get me."

The skull-faced man says, as Skein has heard him say

so many times in the past, "No, this time it's no flash-forward. I'm really here to get you."

"Thank God. Thank God. Thank God."

"Follow along this way. You have your passport handy?"

The familiar words. Skein is prepared to discover he is merely in fugue, and expects to drop back into frustrating reality at any moment. But no. The scene does not waver. It holds firm. It holds. At last he has caught up with this particular scene, overtaking it and enclosing it, pearl-like, in the folds of the present. He is on the way out of the terminal. The skull-faced man helps him through the formalities. How withered he is! How fiery the eyes, how gaunt the face! Those frightening orbits of bone jutting through the skin of the forehead. That parched cheek. Skein listens for a dry rattle of ribs. One sturdy punch and there would be nothing left but a cloud of white dust, slowly settling.

"I know your difficulty," the skull-faced man says. "You've been caught in entropy's jaws. You're being devoured. The injury to your mind—it's tipped you into a situation you aren't able to handle. You *could* handle it, if you'd only learn to adapt to the nature of the perceptions you're getting now. But you won't do that, will you? And you want to be healed. Well, you can be healed here, all right. More or less healed. I'll take you to the place."

"What do you mean, I could handle it, if I'd only learn to adapt?"

"Your injury has liberated you. It's shown you the truth about time. But you refuse to see it."

"What truth?" Skein asks flatly.

"You still try to think that time flows neatly from alpha to omega, from yesterday through today to tomorrow," the skull-faced man says, as they walk slowly through the terminal. "But it doesn't. The idea of the forward flow of time is a deception we impose on ourselves in childhood. An abstraction, agreed upon by common convention, to make it easier for us to cope with phenomena. The truth is that events are random, that chronological flow is only our joint hallucination, that if time can be said to flow at all, it flows in all 'directions' at once. Therefore—"

"Wait," Skein says. "How do you explain the laws of thermodynamics? Entropy increases; available energy constantly diminishes; the universe heads toward ultimate stasis."

"Does it?"

"The second law of thermodynamics—"

"Is an abstraction," the skull-faced man says, "which unfortunately fails to correspond with the situation in the true universe. It isn't a divine law. It's a mathematical hypothesis developed by men who weren't able to perceive the real situation. They did their best to account for the data within a framework they could understand. Their laws are formulations of probability, based on conditions that hold within closed systems, and given the right closed system the second law is useful and illuminating. But in the universe as a whole it simply isn't true. There *is* no arrow of time. Entropy does *not* necessarily increase. Natural processes *can* be reversible. Causes do *not* invariably precede effects. In fact, the concepts of cause and effect are empty. There are neither causes nor effects, but only events, spontaneously generated, which we arrange in our minds in comprehensible patterns of sequence."

"No," Skein mutters. "This is insanity!"

"There are no patterns. Everything is random."

"No."

"Why not admit it? Your brain has been injured; what was destroyed was the center of temporal perception, the node that humans use to impose this unreal order on events. Your time filter has burned out. The past and the future are as accessible to you as the present, Skein: you can go where you like, you can watch events drifting past as they really do. Only you haven't been able to break up your old habits of thought. You still try to impose the conventional entropic order on things, even though you lack the mechanism to do it, now, and the conflict between what you perceive and what you think you perceive is driving you crazy. Eh?"

"How do you know so much about me?"

The skull-faced man chuckles. "I was injured in the same way as you. I was cut free from the time-line long ago, through the kind of overload you suffered. And I've had years to come to terms with the new reality. I was as terrified as you were, at first. But now I understand. I move about freely. I know things, Skein." A rasping laugh. "You need rest, though. A room, a bed. Time to think things over. Come. There's no rush now. You're on the right planet; you'll be all right soon."

Further, the association of entropy increase with time's arrow is in no sense circular; rather, it both tells us something about what will happen to natural systems in time, and about what the time order must be for a series of states of a system. Thus, we may often establish a time order among a set of events by use of the time-entropy association, free from any reference to clocks and magnitudes of time intervals from the present. In actual judgments of before-after we frequently do this on the basis of our experience (even though without any explicit knowledge of the law of entropy increase): we know, for example, that for iron in air the state of pure metal must have been before that of a rusted surface, or that the clothes will be dry after, not before, they have hung in the hot sun.

A tense, humid night of thunder and temporal storms. Lying alone in his oversized hotel room, five kilometers from the purple shore, Skein suffers fiercely from fugue.

"Listen, I have to forbid this. Those turtles are almost extinct. Do you understand that? *Muerto. Perdido. De-*

saparecido. I won't eat a turtle. Throw it back. Throw it back."

"I'm happy to say your second go-round has been approved, Mr. Skein. Not that there was ever any doubt. A long and happy new life to you, sir."

"Go down to it. The force of its power falls off with the cube of the distance; from up here you can't feel it. Go down. Let it take you over. Fuse with it. Make communion, Skein, make communion!"

"Show you the mosyics? Help you understand this marvelous building? A dollar. No? Maybe change money? A good rate."

"First let me get it clear. This man will see everything that's in my mind? He'll get access to my secrets?"

"I love you."
"Get away from me!"

"Won't you ever come to see that causality is merely an illusion, Skein? The notion that there's a consecutive series of events is nothing but a fraud. We impose form on our lives, we talk of time's arrow, we say that there's a flow from A through G and Q to Z, we make believe everything is nicely linear. But it isn't, Skein. It isn't."

Breakfast on a leafy veranda. Morning light out of the west, making the trees glow with an ultramarine glitter. The skull-faced man joins him. Skein secretly searches the parched face. Is everything an illusion? Perhaps *he* is an illusion.

They walk toward the sea. Well before noon they reach the shore. The skull-faced man points to the south, and they follow the coast; it is often a difficult hike, for in places the sand is washed out and they must detour inland, scrambling over quartzy cliffs. The monstrous old man is indefatigable. When they pause to rest, squatting on a timeless purple strand made smooth by the recent tide, the debate about time resumes, and Skein hears words that have been echoing in his skull for four years and more. It is as though everything up till now has been a rehearsal for a play, and now at last he has taken the stage.

"Won't you ever come to see that causality is merely an illusion, Skein?"

"I feel an obligation to awaken your mind to the truth."

"Time is an ocean, and events come drifting to us as randomly as dead animals on the waves."

Skein offers all the proper cues.

"I won't accept that! It's a demonic, chaotic, nihilistic theory."

"You can say that after all you've experienced?"

"I'll go on saying it. What I've been going through is a mental illness. Maybe I'm deranged, but the universe isn't."

"Contrary. You've only recently become sane and started to see things as they really are. The trouble is that you don't want to admit the evidence you've begun to perceive. Your filters are down, Skein! You've shaken free of the illusion of linearity! Now's your chance to show your resilience. Learn to live with the real reality. Stop this silly business of imposing an artificial order on the flow of time. Why *should* effect follow cause? Why *shouldn't* the seed follow the tree? Why must you persist in holding tight to a useless, outworn, contemptible system of false evaluations of experience when you've managed to break free of the—"

"Stop it! Stop it! Stop it! Stop it!"

By early afternoon they are many kilometers from the hotel, still keeping as close to the shore as they can. The terrain is uneven and divided, with rugged fingers of rock running almost to the water's edge, and Skein finds the journey even more exhausting than it had seemed in his visions of it. Several times he stops, panting, and has to be urged to go on.

"It isn't much farther," the skull-faced man says. "You can make it. Step by step is how."

"I'm winded. Those hills—"

"I'm twice your age, and I'm doing fine."

"You're in better shape. I've been cooped up on spaceships for months and months."

"Just a short way on," says the skull-faced man. "About a hundred meters from the shore."

Skein struggles on. The heat is frightful. He trips in the sand; he is blinded by sweat; he has a momentary flashback fugue. "There it is," the skull-faced man says, finally. "Look there, in the pit."

Skein beholds the conical crater. He sees the golden amoeba.

"Go down to it," the skull-faced man says. "The force of its power falls off with the cube of the distance; from up here you can't feel it. Go down. Let it take you over. Fuse with it. Make communion, Skein, make communion!"

"And will it heal me? So that I'll function as I did before the trouble started?"

"If you let it heal you, it will. That's what it wants to do. It's a completely benign organism. It thrives on repairing broken souls. Let it into your head; let it find the damaged place. You can trust it. Go down."

Skein trembles on the edge of the pit. The creature below flows and eddies, becoming first long and narrow, then high and squat, then resuming its basically circular form. Its color deepens almost to scarlet, and its radiance shifts toward yellow. As if preening and stretching itself. It seems to be waiting for him. It seems eager. This is what he has sought so long, going from planet to wearying planet. The skull-faced man, the purple sand, the pit, the creature. Skein slips his sandals off. *What have I to lose?* He sits for a moment on the pit's rim; then he shimmies down, sliding part of the way, and lands softly, close beside the being that awaits him. And immediately feels its power. Something brushes against his brain. The sensation reminds him of the training sessions of his first go-round, when the instructors were showing him how to develop his gift. The fingers probing his consciousness. Go on, enter, he tells them. I'm open. I'm open. And he finds himself in contact with the being of the pit. Wordless. A two-way flow of unintelligible images is the only communion; shapes drift from and into his mind. The universe blurs. He is no longer sure where the center of his ego lies. He has thought of his brain as a sphere with himself at its center, but now it seems extended, elliptical, and an ellipse has no center, only a pair of foci, here and here, one focus in his own skull and one—where?—within that fleshy amoeba. And suddenly he is looking at himself through the amoeba's eyes. The large biped with the bony body. How strange, how grotesque! Yet it suffers. Yet it must be helped. It is injured. It is broken. We go to it with all our love. We will heal. And Skein feels something flowing over the bare folds and fissures of his brain. But he can no longer remember whether he is the human or the alien, the bony one or the boneless. Their identities have mingled. He goes through fugues by the scores, seeing yesterdays and tomorrows, and everything is formless and without content; he is unable to recognize himself or to understand the words being spoken. It does not matter. All is random. All is illusion. Release the knot of pain you clutch within you. Accept. Accept. Accept. Accept.

He accepts.

He releases.

He merges.

He casts away the shreds of ego, the constricting exoskeleton of self, and placidly permits the necessary adjustments to be made.

The possibility, however, of genuine thermodynamic entropy decrease for an isolated system—no matter how rare—does raise an objection to the definition of time's direction in terms of entropy. If a large, isolated system did by chance go through an entropy decrease as one state evolved from another, we would have to say that time "went backward" if our definition of time's arrow were basically in terms of entropy increase. But with an ultimate definition of the forward direction of time in terms of the actual occurrence of states, and measured time intervals from the present, we can readily accommodate the entropy decrease; it would become merely a rare anomaly in the physical processes of the natural world.

The wind is rising. The sand, blown aloft, stains the sky gray. Skein clambers from the pit and lies by its rim, breathing hard. The skull-faced man helps him get up.

Skein has seen this series of images hundreds of times.

"How do you feel?" the skull-faced man asks.

"Strange. Good. My head seems to clear!"

"You had communion down there?"

"Oh, yes. Yes."

"And?"

"I think I'm healed," Skein says in wonder. "My strength is back. Before, you know, I felt cut down to the bone, a minimum version of myself. And now. And now." He lets a tendril of consciousness slip forth. It meets the mind of the skull-faced man. Skein is aware of a glassy interface; he can touch the other mind, but he cannot enter it. "Are you a Communicator too?" Skein asks, awed.

"In a sense. I feel you touching me. You're better, aren't you?"

"Much. Much. Much."

"As I told you. Now you have your second chance,

Skein. Your gift has been restored. Courtesy of our friend in the pit. They love being helpful."

"What shall I do now? Where shall I go?"

"Anything. Anywhere. Anywhen. You're free to move along the time-line as you please. In a state of controlled, directed fugue, so to speak. After all, if time is random, if there is no rigid sequence of events——"

"Yes."

"Then why not choose the sequence that appeals to you? Why stick to the set of abstractions your former self has handed you? You're a free man, Skein. Go. Enjoy. Undo your past. Edit it. Improve on it. It isn't your past, any more than this is your present. It's all one, Skein, all *one*. Pick the segment you prefer."

He tests the truth of the skull-faced man's words. Cautiously Skein steps three minutes into the past and sees himself struggling up out of the pit. He slides four minutes into the future and sees the skull-faced man, alone, trudging northward along the shore. Everything flows. All is fluidity. He is free. He is free.

"You see, Skein?"

"Now I do," Skein says. He is out of entropy's jaws. He is time's master, which is to say he is his own master. He can move at will. He can defy the imaginary forces of determinism. Suddenly he realizes what he must do now. He will assert his free will; he will challenge entropy on its home ground. Skein smiles. He cuts free of the time-line and floats easily into what others would call the past.

"Get Nissenson into a receptive state," he orders his desk.

Coustakis, blinking rapidly, obviously uneasy, says, "First let me get it clear. This man will see everything that's in my mind? He'll get access to my secrets?"

"No. No. I filter the communion with great care. Nothing will pass from your mind to his except the nature of the problem you want him to tackle. Nothing will come back from his mind to yours except the answer."

"And if he doesn't have the answer?"

"He will."

"And if he goes into the transmission business for himself afterward?" Coustakis asks.

"He's bonded," Skein says curtly. "No chance of it. Let's go, now. Up and together."

The desk reports that Nissenson, half the world away in São Paulo, is ready. Quickly Skein throws Coustakis into the receptive condition, and swings around to face the brilliant lights of his data-access units. Here is the moment when he can halt the transaction. Turn again, Skein. Face Coustakis, smile sadly, inform him that the communion will be impossible. Give him back his money, send him off to break some other Communicator's mind. And live on, whole and happy, ever after. It was at this point, visiting this scene endlessly in his fugues, that Skein silently and hopelessly cried out to himself to stop. Now it is within his power, for this is no fugue, no illusion of time-shift. He has shifted. He is here, carrying with him the knowledge of all that is to come, and he is the only Skein on the scene, the operative Skein. Get up, now. Refuse the contract.

He does not. Thus he defies entropy. Thus he breaks the chain.

He peers into the sparkling, shifting little blazes until they kindle his gift, jabbing at the electrical rhythms of his brain until he is lifted into the energy level that permits the opening of a communion. He starts to go up. He reaches forth one tendril of his mind and engages Nissenson. With another tendril he snares Coustakis. Steadily, now, he draws the two tendrils together. He is aware of the risks, but believes he can surmount them.

The tendrils meet.

Out of Coustakis' mind flows a description of the matter transmitter and a clear statement of the beam-spread problem; Skein shoves it along to Nissenson, who begins to work on a solution. The combined strength of the two minds is great, but Skein deftly lets the excess charge bleed away, and maintains the communion with no particular effort, holding Coustakis and Nissenson together while they deal with their technical matters. Skein pays little attention as their excited minds rush toward answers. *If you. Yes, and then. But if. I see, yes. I could. And. However, maybe I should. I like that. It leads to. Of course. The inevitable result. Is it feasible, though? I think so. You might have to. I could. Yes. I could. I could.*

"I thank you a million times," Coustakis says to Skein. "It was all so simple, once we saw how we ought to look at it. I don't begrudge your fee at all. Not at all."

Coustakis leaves, glowing with delight. Skein, relieved, tells his desk, "I'm going to allow myself a three-day holiday. Fix the schedule to move everybody up accordingly."

He smiles. He strides across his office, turning up the amplifiers, treating himself to the magnificent view. The nightmare undone. The past revised. The burnout avoided. All it took was confidence. Enlightenment. A proper understanding of the processes involved.

He feels the sudden swooping sensations of incipient temporal fugue. Before he can intervene to regain control, he swings off into darkness and arrives instantaneously on a planet of purple sand and blue-leaved trees. Orange waves lap at the shore. He stands a few meters from a deep conical pit. Peering into it, he sees an amoebalike creature lying beside a human figure; strands of the alien's jellylike substance are wound around the man's body. He recognizes the man to be John Skein. The communion in the pit ends; the man begins to clamber from the pit. The wind is rising. The sand, blown aloft, stains the sky gray. Patiently he watches his younger self struggling up from the pit. Now he understands. The circuit is closed; the knot is tied; the identity loop is complete. He is destined to spend many years on Abbondanza VI, growing ancient and withered. He is the skull-faced man.

Skein reaches the rim of the pit and lies there, breathing hard. He helps Skein get up.

"How do you feel?" he asks.

The Reality Trip

I am a reclamation project for her. She lives on my floor of the hotel, a dozen rooms down the hall: a lady poet, private income. No, that makes her sound too old, a middle-aged eccentric. Actually she is no more than thirty. Taller than I am, with long kinky brown hair and a sharp, bony nose that has a bump on the bridge. Eyes are very glossy. A studied raggedness about her dress; carefully chosen shabby clothes. I am in no position really to judge the sexual attractiveness of Earthfolk but I gather from remarks made by men living here that she is not considered good-looking. I pass her often on my way to my room. She smiles fiercely at me. Saying to herself, no doubt, You poor lonely man. Let me help you bear the burden of your unhappy life. Let me show you the meaning of love, for I too know what it is like to be alone.

Or words to that effect. She's never actually said any such thing. But her intentions are transparent. When she sees me, a kind of hunger comes into her eyes, part maternal, part (I guess) sexual, and her face takes on a wild crazy intensity. Burning with emotion. Her name is Elizabeth Cooke. "Are you fond of poetry, Mr. Knecht?" she asked me this morning, as we creaked upward together in the ancient elevator. And an hour later she

47

knocked at my door. "Something for you to read," she said. "I wrote them." A sheaf of large yellow sheets, stapled at the top; poems printed in smeary blue mimeography. *The Reality Trip*, the collection was headed. *Limited Edition: 125 Copies.* "You can keep it if you like," she explained. "I've got lots more." She was wearing bright corduroy slacks and a flimsy pink shawl through which her breasts plainly showed. Small tapering breasts, not very functional-looking. When she saw me studying them her nostrils flared momentarily and she blinked her eyes three times swiftly. Tokens of lust?

I read the poems. Is it fair for me to offer judgment on them? Even though I've lived on this planet eleven of its years, even though my command of colloquial English is quite good, do I really comprehend the inner life of poetry? I thought they were all quite bad. Earnest, plodding poems, capturing what they call slices of life. The world around her, the cruel, brutal, unloving city. Lamenting the failure of people to open to one another. The title poem began this way:

> *He was on the reality trip. Big black man,*
> *bloodshot eyes, bad teeth. Eisenhower jacket,*
> *frayed. Smell of cheap wine. I guess a knife*
> *in his pocket. Looked at me mean. Criminal*
> *record. Rape, child-beating, possession of drugs.*
> *In his head saying, slavemistress bitch, and me in*
> *my head saying, black brother, let's freak in to-*
> *gether, let's trip on love—*

And so forth. Warm, direct emotion; but is the urge to love all wounded things a sufficient center for poetry? I don't know. I did put her poems through the scanner and transmit them to Homeworld, although I doubt they'll learn much from them about Earth. It would flatter Elizabeth to know that while she has few readers here, she has acquired some ninety light-years away. But of course I can't tell her that.

She came back a short while ago. "Did you like them?" she asked.

"Very much. You have such sympathy for those who suffer."

I think she expected me to invite her in. I was careful not to look at her breasts this time.

* * *

The hotel is on West 23rd Street. It must be over a hundred years old; the façade is practically baroque and the interior shows a kind of genteel decay. The place has a bohemian tradition. Most of its guests are permanent residents and many of them are artists, novelists, playwrights, and such. I have lived here nine years. I know a number of the residents by name, and they me, but I have discouraged any real intimacy, naturally, and everyone has respected that choice. I do not invite others into my room. Sometimes I let myself be invited to visit theirs, since one of my responsibilities on this world is to get to know something of the way Earthfolk live and think. Elizabeth is the first to attempt to cross the invisible barrier of privacy I surround myself with. I'm not sure how I'll handle that. She moved in about three years ago; her attentions became noticeable perhaps ten months back, and for the last five or six weeks she's been a great nuisance. Some kind of confrontation is inevitable: either I must tell her to leave me alone, or I will find myself drawn into a situation impossible to tolerate. Perhaps she'll find someone else to feel even sorrier for, before it comes to that.

My daily routine rarely varies. I rise at seven. First Feeding. Then I clean my skin (my outer one, the Earthskin, I mean) and dress. From eight to ten I transmit data to Homeworld. Then I go out for the morning field trip: talking to people, buying newspapers, often some library research. At one I return to my room. Second Feeding. I transmit data from two to five. Out again, perhaps to the theater, to a motion picture, to a political meeting. I must soak up the flavor of this planet. Often to saloons; I am equipped for ingesting alcohol, though of course I must get rid of it before it has been in my body very long, and I drink and listen and sometimes argue. At midnight back to my room. Third Feeding. Transmit data from one to four in the morning. Then three hours of sleep, and at seven the cycle begins anew. It is a comforting schedule. I don't know how many agents Homeworld has on Earth, but I like to think that I'm one of the most diligent and useful. I miss very little. I've done good service, and, as they say here, hard work is its own reward. I won't deny that I hate the physical discomfort of it and frequently give way to real despair over my isolation from my own kind. Sometimes I even think of asking for a transfer to Homeworld. But what would become of me there? What services could I perform? I have shaped my life to one end: that of dwelling among the Earthfolk and reporting on their ways. If I give that up, I am nothing.

* * *

Of course there is the physical pain. Which is considerable.

The gravitational pull of Earth is almost twice that of Homeworld. It makes for a leaden life for me. My inner organs always sagging against the lower rim of my carapace. My muscles cracking with strain. Every movement a willed effort. My heart in constant protest. In my eleven years I have as one might expect adapted somewhat to the conditions; I have toughened, I have thickened. I suspect that if I were transported instantly to Homeworld now I would be quite giddy, baffled by the lightness of everything. I would leap and soar and stumble, and might even miss this crushing pull of Earth. Yet I doubt that. I suffer here; at all times the weight oppresses me. Not to sound too self-pitying about it. I knew the conditions in advance. I was placed in simulated Earth gravity when I volunteered, and was given a chance to withdraw, and I decided to go anyway. Not realizing that a week under double gravity is not the same thing as a lifetime. I could always have stepped out of the simulation chamber. Not here. The eternal drag on every molecule of me. The pressure. My flesh is always in mourning.

And the outer body I must wear. This cunning disguise. Forever to be swaddled in thick masses of synthetic flesh, smothering me, engulfing me. The soft slippery slap of it against the self within. The elaborate framework that holds it erect, by which I make it move: a forest of struts and braces and servoactuators and cables, in the midst of which I must unendingly huddle, atop my little platform in the gut. Adopting one or another of various uncomfortable positions, constantly shifting and squirming, now jabbing myself on some awkwardly placed projection, now trying to make my inflexible body flexibly to bend. Seeing the world by periscope through mechanical eyes. Enwombed in this mountain of meat. It is a clever thing; it must look convincingly human, since no one has ever doubted me, and it ages ever so slightly from year to year, graying a bit at the temples, thickening a bit at the paunch. It walks. It talks. It takes in food and drink, when it has to. (And deposits them in a removable pouch near my leftmost arm.) And I within it. The hidden chess player; the invisible rider. If I dared, I would periodically strip myself of this cloak of flesh and crawl around my room in my own guise. But it is forbidden. Eleven years now and I have not been outside my protoplasmic housing. I feel sometimes that it has come to adhere to me, that it is no longer merely around me but by now a part of me.

In order to eat I must unseal it at the middle, a process that takes many minutes. Three times a day I unbutton myself so that I can stuff the food concentrates into my true gullet. Faulty design, I call that. They could just as easily have arranged it so I could pop the food into my Earthmouth and have it land in my own digestive tract. I suppose the newer models have that. Excretion is just as troublesome for me; I unseal, reach in, remove the cubes of waste, seal my skin again. Down the toilet with them. A nuisance.

And the loneliness! To look at the stars and know Homeworld is out there somewhere! To think of all the others, mating, chanting, dividing, abstracting, while I live out my days in this crumbling hotel on an alien planet, tugged down by gravity and locked within a cramped counterfeit body—always alone, always pretending that I am not what I am and that I am what I am not, spying, questioning, recording, reporting, coping with the misery of solitude, hunting for the comforts of philosophy—

In all of this there is only one real consolation, aside, that is, from the pleasure of knowing that I am of service to Homeworld. The atmosphere of New York City grows grimier every year. The streets are full of crude vehicles belching undigested hydrocarbons. To the Earthfolk, this stuff is pollution, and they mutter worriedly about it. To me it is joy. It is the only touch of Homeworld here: that sweet soup of organic compounds adrift in the air. It intoxicates me. I walk down the street breathing deeply, sucking the good molecules through my false nostrils to my authentic lungs. The natives must think I'm insane. Tripping on auto exhaust! Can I get arrested for over-enthusiastic public breathing? Will they pull me in for a mental checkup?

*   *   *

Elizabeth Cooke continues to waft wistful attentions at me. Smiles in the hallway. Hopeful gleam of the eyes. "Perhaps we can have dinner together some night soon, Mr. Knecht. I know we'd have so much to talk about. And maybe you'd like to see the new poems I've been doing." She is trembling. Eyelids flickering tensely; head held rigid on long neck. I know she sometimes has men in her room, so it can't be out of loneliness or frustration that she's cultivating me. And I doubt that she's sexually attracted to my outer self. I believe I'm being accurate when I say that women don't consider me sexually magnetic. No, she loves me because she pities me. The sad shy bachelor at the end of the hall, dear unhappy Mr. Knecht; can I bring some brightness into his dreary life? And so forth. I think that's how it is. Will I be able to go on avoiding her? Perhaps I should move to another part of the city. But I've lived here so long; I've grown accustomed to this hotel. Its easy ways do much to compensate for the hardships of my post. And my familiar room. The huge many-paned window; the cracked green floor tiles in the bathroom; the lumpy patterns of replastering on the wall above my bed. The high ceiling; the funny chandelier. Things that I love. But of course I can't let her try to start an affair with me. We are supposed to observe Earthfolk, not to get involved with them. Our disguise is not that difficult to penetrate at close range. I must keep her away somehow. Or flee.

*   *   *

Incredible! There is another of us in this very hotel!
As I learned through accident. At one this afternoon,

returning from my morning travels: Elizabeth in the lobby, as though lying in wait for me, chatting with the manager. Rides up with me in the elevator. Her eyes looking into mine. "Sometimes I think you're afraid of me," she begins. "You mustn't be. That's the great tragedy of human life, that people shut themselves up behind walls of fear and never let anyone through, anyone who might care about them and be warm to them. You've got no reason to be afraid of me." I do, but how to explain that to her? To sidestep prolonged conversation and possible entanglement I get off the elevator one floor below the right one. Let her think I'm visiting a friend. Or a mistress. I walk slowly down the hall to the stairs, using up time, waiting so she will be in her room before I go up. A maid bustles by me. She thrusts her key into a door on the left: a rare *faux pas* for the usually competent help here, she forgets to knock before going in to make up the room. The door opens and the occupant, inside, stands revealed. A stocky, muscular man, naked to the waist. "Oh, excuse me," the maid gasps, and backs out, shutting the door. But I have seen. My eyes are quick. The hairy chest is split, a dark gash three inches wide and some eleven inches long, beginning between the nipples and going past the navel. Visible within is the black shiny surface of a Homeworld carapace. My countryman, opening up for Second Feeding. Dazed, numbed, I stagger to the stairs and pull myself step by leaden step to my floor. No sign of Elizabeth. I stumble into my room and throw the bolt. Another of us here? Well, why not? I'm not the only one. There may be hundreds in New York alone. But in the same hotel? I remember, now, I've seen him occasionally: a silent, dour man, tense, hunted-looking, unsociable. No doubt I appear the same way to others. Keep the world at a distance. I don't know his name or what he is supposed to do for a living.

We are forbidden to make contact with fellow Homeworlders except in case of extreme emergency. Isolation is a necessary condition of our employment. I may not introduce myself to him; I may not seek his friendship. It is worse now for me, knowing that he is here, than when I was entirely alone. The things we could reminisce about! The friends we might have in common! We could reinforce one another's endurance of the gravity, the discomfort of our disguises, the vile climate. But no. I must pretend I know nothing. The rules. The harsh, unbending rules. I to go about my business, he his; if we meet, no hint of my knowledge must pass.

So be it. I will honor my vows. But it may be difficult.

* * *

He goes by the name of Swanson. Been living in the hotel eighteen months; a musician of some sort, according to the manager. "A very peculiar man. Keeps to himself; no small talk, never smiles. Defends his privacy. The other day a maid barged into his room without knocking and I thought he'd sue. Well, we get all sorts here." The manager thinks he may actually be a member of one of the old European royal families, living in exile, or something similarly romantic. The manager would be surprised.

* * *

I defend my privacy too. From Elizabeth, another assault on it.

In the hall outside my room. "My new poems," she said. "In case you're interested." And then: "Can I come in? I'd read them to you. I love reading out loud." And: "Please don't always seem so terribly afraid of me. I don't bite, David. Really I don't. I'm quite gentle."

"I'm sorry."

"So am I." Anger, now, lurking in her shiny eyes, her thin taut lips. "If you want me to leave you alone, say so, I will. But I want you to know how cruel you're being. I don't *demand* anything from you. I'm just offering some friendship. And you're refusing. Do I have a bad smell? Am I so ugly? Is it my poems you hate and you're afraid to tell me?"

"Elizabeth—"

"We're only on this world such a short time. Why can't we be kinder to each other while we are? To love, to share, to open up. The reality trip. Communication, soul to soul." Her tone changed. An artful shading. "For all I know, women turn you off. I wouldn't put anybody down for that. We've all got our ways. But it doesn't have to be a sexual thing, you and me. Just talk. Like, opening the channels. Please? Say no and I'll never bother you again, but don't say no, please. That's like shutting a door on life, David. And when you do that, you start to die a little."

Persistent. I should tell her to go to hell. But there is the loneliness. There is her obvious sincerity. Her warmth, her eagerness to pull me from my lunar isolation. Can there be harm in it? Knowing that Swanson is nearby, so close yet sealed from me by iron commandments, has intensified my sense of being alone. I can risk letting Elizabeth get closer to me. It will make her happy; it may make me happy; it could even yield information valuable to Homeworld. Of course I must still maintain certain barriers.

"I don't mean to be unfriendly. I think you've misunderstood, Elizabeth. I haven't really been rejecting you. Come in. Do come in." Stunned, she enters my room. The first guest ever. My few books; my modest furnishings; the ultrawave transmitter, impenetrably disguised as a piece of sculpture. She sits. Skirt far above the knees. Good legs, if I understand the criteria of quality correctly. I am determined to allow no sexual overtures. If she tries anything, I'll resort to—I don't know—hysteria. "Read me your new poems," I say. She opens her portfolio. Reads.

> *In the midst of the hipster night of doubt and*
> *Emptiness, when the bad-trip god came to me with.*
> *Cold hands, I looked up and shouted yes at the*
> *Stars. And yes and yes again. I groove on yes;*
> *The devil grooves on no. And I waited for you to*
> *Say yes, and at last you did. And the world said*
> *The stars said the trees said the grass said the*
> *Sky said the streets said yes and yes and yes—*

She is ecstatic. Her face is flushed; her eyes are joyous. She has broken through to me. After two hours, when it becomes obvious that I am not going to ask her to go to bed with me, she leaves. Not to wear out her welcome. "I'm so glad I was wrong about you, David," she whispers. "I couldn't believe you were really a life-denier. And you're not." Ecstatic.

* * *

I am getting into very deep water.

We spend an hour or two together every night. Sometimes in my room, sometimes in hers. Usually she comes to me, but now and then, to be polite, I seek her out after Third Feeding. By now I've read all her poetry; we talk instead of the arts in general, politics, racial problems. She has a lively, well-stocked, disorderly mind. Though she probes constantly for information about me, she realizes how sensitive I am, and quickly withdraws when I parry her. Asking about my work; I reply vaguely that I'm doing research for a book, and when I don't amplify she drops it, though she tries again, gently, a few nights later. She drinks a lot of wine, and offers it to me. I nurse one glass through a whole visit. Often she suggests we go out together for dinner; I explain that I have digestive problems and prefer to eat alone, and she takes this in good grace but immediately resolves to help me overcome those problems, for soon she is asking me to eat with her again. There is an excellent Spanish restaurant right in the hotel, she says. She drops troublesome questions. Where was I born? Did I go to college? Do I have family somewhere? Have I ever been married? Have I published any of my writings? I improvise evasions. Nothing difficult about that, except that never before have I allowed anyone on Earth such sustained contact with me, so prolonged an opportunity to find inconsistencies in my pretended identity. What if she sees through?

And sex. Her invitations grow less subtle. She seems to think that we ought to be having a sexual relationship, simply because we've become such good friends. Not a matter of passion so much as one of communication: we talk, sometimes we take walks together, we should do *that* together too. But of course it's impossible. I have the external organs but not the capacity to use them. Wouldn't want her touching my false skin in any case. How to deflect her? If I declare myself impotent she'll demand a chance to try to cure me. If I pretend homosexuality she'll start some kind of straightening therapy. If I simply say she doesn't turn me on physically she'll be hurt. The sexual thing is a challenge to her, the way merely getting me to talk with her once was. She often wears the transparent pink shawl that reveals her breasts. Her skirts are hip-high. She doses herself with aphrodisiac perfumes. She grazes my body with hers whenever opportunity arises. The tension mounts; she is determined to have me.

I have said nothing about her in my reports to Homeworld. Though I do transmit some of the psychological data I have gathered by observing her.

"Could you ever admit you were in love with me?" she asked tonight.

And she asked, "Doesn't it hurt you to repress your feelings all the time? To sit there locked up inside yourself like a prisoner?"

And, "There's a physical side of life too, David. I don't mind so much the damage you're doing to me by ignoring it. But I worry about the damage you're doing to you."

Crossing her legs. Hiking her skirt even higher.

We are heading toward a crisis. I should never have let this begin. A torrid summer has descended on the city, and in hot weather my nervous system is always at the edge of eruption. She may push me too far. I might ruin everything. I should apply for transfer to Homeworld before I cause trouble. Maybe I should confer with Swanson. I think what is happening now qualifies as an emergency.

Elizabeth stayed past midnight tonight. I had to ask her finally to leave: work to do. An hour later she pushed an envelope under my door. Newest poems. Love poems. In a shaky hand: *David you mean so much to me. You mean the stars and nebulas. Cant you let me show my love? Cant you accept happiness? Think about it. I adore you.*

What have I started?

* * *

103°F. today. The fourth successive day of intolerable heat. Met Swanson in the elevator at lunch time; nearly blurted the truth about myself to him. I must be more careful. But my control is slipping. Last night, in the worst of the heat, I was tempted to strip off my disguise. I could no longer stand being locked in here, pivoting and ducking to avoid all the machinery festooned about me. Resisted the temptation; just barely. Somehow I am more sensitive to the gravity too. I have the illusion that my carapace is developing cracks. Almost collapsed in the street this afternoon. All I need: heat exhaustion, whisked off to the hospital, routine fluoroscope exam. "You have a very odd skeletal structure, Mr. Knecht." Indeed. Dissecting me, next, with three thousand medical students looking on. And then the United Nations called in. Menace from outer space. Yes. I must be more careful. I must be more careful. I must be more—

* * *

Now I've done it. Eleven years of faithful service destroyed in a single wild moment. Violation of the Fundamental Rule. I hardly believe it. How was it possible that I—that I—with my respect for my responsibilities —that I could have—even considered, let alone actually done—

But the weather was terribly hot. The third week of the heat wave. I was stifling inside my false body. And the gravity: was New York having a gravity wave too? That terrible pull, worse than ever. Bending my internal organs out of shape. Elizabeth a tremendous annoyance: passionate, emotional, teary, poetic, giving me no rest, pleading for me to burn with a brighter flame. Declaring her love in sonnets, in rambling hip epics, in haiku. Spending two hours in my room, crouched at my feet, murmuring about the hidden beauty of my soul. "Open yourself and let love come in," she whispered. "It's like giving yourself to God. Making a commitment; breaking down all walls. Why not? For love's sake, David, why not?" I couldn't tell her why not, and she went away, but about midnight she was back knocking at my door. I let her in. She wore an ankle-length silk housecoat, gleaming, threadbare. "I'm stoned," she said hoarsely, voice an octave too deep. "I had to bust three joints to get up the nerve. But here I am. David, I'm sick of making the turnoff trip. We've been so wonderfully close, and then you won't go the last stretch of the way." A cascade of giggles. "Tonight you will. Don't fail me. Darling." Drops the housecoat. Naked underneath it: narrow waist, bony hips, long legs, thin thighs, blue veins crossing her breasts. Her hair wild and kinky. A sorceress. A seeress. Berserk. Approaching me, eyes slit-wide, mouth open, tongue flickering snakily. How fleshless she is! Beads of sweat glistening on her flat chest. Seizes my wrists; tugs me roughly toward the bed. We tussle a little. Within my false body I throw switches, nudge levers. I am stronger than she is. I pull free, breaking her hold with an effort. She stands flat-footed in front of me, glaring, eyes fiery. So vulnerable, so sad in her nudity. And yet so fierce. "David! David! David!" Sobbing. Breathless. Pleading with her eyes and the tips of her breasts. Gathering her strength; now she makes the next lunge, but I see it coming and let her topple past me. She lands on the bed, burying her face in the pillow, clawing at the sheet. "Why? Why why why WHY?" she screams.

In a minute we will have the manager in here. With the police.

"Am I so hideous? I love you, David, do you know what that word means? Love. Love." Sits up. Turns to me. Imploring. "Don't reject me," she whispers. "I couldn't take that. You know, I just wanted to make you happy, I figured I could be the one, only I didn't realize how unhappy you'd make me. And you just stand there. And you don't say anything. What are you, some kind of machine?"

"I'll tell you what I am," I said.

That was when I went sliding into the abyss. All control lost; all prudence gone. My mind so slathered with raw emotion that survival itself means nothing. I must make things clear to her, is all. I must show her. At whatever expense. I strip off my shirt. She glows, no doubt thinking I will let myself be seduced. My hands slide up and down my bare chest, seeking the catches

and snaps. I go through the intricate, cumbersome process of opening my body. Deep within myself something
is shouting NO NO NO NO NO, but I pay no attention.
The heart has its reasons.

Hoarsely: "Look, Elizabeth. Look at me. This is what
I am. Look at me and freak out. The reality trip."

My chest opens wide.

I push myself forward, stepping between the levers
and struts, emerging halfway from the human shell I
wear. I have not been this far out of it since the day
they sealed me in, on Homeworld. I let her see my
gleaming carapace. I wave my eyestalks around. I allow
some of my claws to show. "See? See? Big black crab
from outer space. That's what you love, Elizabeth. That's
what I am. David Knecht's just a costume, and this is
what's inside it." I have gone insane. "You want reality?
Here's reality, Elizabeth. What good is the Knecht body
to you? It's a fraud. It's a machine. Come on, come
closer. Do you want to kiss me? Should I get on you and
make love?"

During this episode her face has displayed an amazing
range of reactions. Open-mouthed disbelief at first, of
course. And frozen horror: gagging sounds in throat,
jaws agape, eyes wide and rigid. Hands fanned across
breasts. Sudden modesty in front of the alien monster?
But then, as the familiar Knecht-voice, now bitter and
impassioned, continues to flow from the black thing within the sundered chest, a softening of her response. Curiosity. The poetic sensibility taking over. Nothing human
is alien to me: Terence, quoted by Cicero. Nothing alien
is alien to me. Eh? She will accept the evidence of her
eyes. "What are you? Where did you come from?" And I
say, "I've violated the Fundamental Rule. I deserve to
be plucked and thinned. We're not supposed to reveal
ourselves. If we get into some kind of accident that might
lead to exposure, we're supposed to blow ourselves up.
The switch is right here." She comes close and peers
around me, into the cavern of David Knecht's chest.

"From some other planet? Living here in disguise?" She understands the picture. Her shock is fading. She even laughs. "I've seen worse than you on acid," she says. "You don't frighten me now, David. David? Shall I go on calling you David?"

This is unreal and dreamlike to me. I have revealed myself, thinking to drive her away in terror; she is no longer aghast, and smiles at my strangeness. She kneels to get a better look. I move back a short way. Eyestalks fluttering: I am uneasy, I have somehow lost the upper hand in this encounter.

She says, "I knew you were unusual, but not like this. But it's all right. I can cope. I mean, the essential personality, that's what I fell in love with. Who cares that you're a crab-man from the Green Galaxy? Who cares that we can't ever be real lovers? I can make that sacrifice. It's your soul I dig, David. Go on. Close yourself up again. You don't look comfortable this way." The triumph of love. She will not abandon me, even now. Disaster. I crawl back into Knecht and lift his arms to his chest to seal it. Shock is glazing my consciousness: the enormity, the audacity. What have I done? Elizabeth watches, awed, even delighted. At last I am together again. She nods. "Listen," she tells me, "You can trust me. I mean, if you're some kind of spy, checking out the Earth, I don't care. *I don't care.* I won't tell anybody. Pour it all out, David. Tell me about yourself. Don't you see, this is the biggest thing that ever happened to me. A chance to show that love isn't just physical, isn't just chemistry, that it's a soul trip, that it crosses not just racial lines but the lines of the whole damned species, the planet itself—"

*   *   *

It took several hours to get rid of her. A soaring, intense conversation, Elizabeth doing most of the talking.

She putting forth theories of why I had come to Earth, me nodding, denying, amplifying, mostly lost in horror at my own perfidy and barely listening to her monolog. And the humidity turning me into rotting rags. Finally: "I'm down from the pot, David. And all wound up. I'm going out for a walk. Then back to my room to write for a while. To put this night into a poem before I lose the power of it. But I'll come to you again by dawn, all right? That's maybe five hours from now. You'll be here? You won't do anything foolish? Oh, I love you so much, David! Do you believe me? Do you?"

When she was gone I stood a long while by the window, trying to reassemble myself. Shattered. Drained. Remembering her kisses, her lips running along the ridge marking the place where my chest opens. The fascination of the abomination. She will love me even if I am crustaceous beneath.

I had to have help.

I went to Swanson's room. He was slow to respond to my knock; busy transmitting, no doubt. I could hear him within, but he didn't answer. "Swanson?" I called. "Swanson?" Then I added the distress signal in the Homeworld tongue. He rushed to the door. Blinking, suspicious. "It's all right," I said. "Look, let me in. I'm in big trouble." Speaking English, but I gave him the distress signal again.

"How did you know about me?" he asked.

"The day the maid blundered into your room while you were eating, I was going by. I saw."

"But you aren't supposed to—"

"Except in emergencies. This is an emergency." He shut off his ultrawave and listened intently to my story. Scowling. He didn't approve. But he wouldn't spurn me. I had been criminally foolish, but I was of his kind, prey to the same pains, the same lonelinesses, and he would help me.

"What do you plan to do now?" he asked. "You can't harm her. It isn't allowed."

"I don't want to harm her. Just to get free of her. To make her fall out of love with me."

"How? If showing yourself to her didn't—"

"Infidelity," I said. "Making her see that I love someone else. No room in my life for her. That'll drive her away. Afterwards it won't matter that she knows: who'd believe her story? The FBI would laugh and tell her to lay off the LSD. But if I don't break her attachment to me I'm finished."

"Love someone else? Who?"

"When she comes back to my room at dawn," I said, "she'll find the two of us together, dividing and abstracting. I think that'll do it, don't you?"

* * *

So I deceived Elizabeth with Swanson.

The fact that we both wore male human identities was irrelevant, of course. We went to my room and stepped out of our disguises—a bold, dizzying sensation!—and suddenly we were just two Homeworlders again, receptive to one another's needs. I left the door unlocked. Swanson and I crawled up on my bed and began the chanting. How strange it was, after these years of solitude, to feel those vibrations again! And how beautiful. Swanson's vibrissae touching mine. The interplay of harmonies. An underlying sternness to his technique—he was contemptuous of me for my idiocy, and rightly so—but once we passed from the chanting to the dividing all was forgiven, and as we moved into the abstracting it was truly sublime. We climbed through an infinity of climactic emptyings. Dawn crept upon us and found us unwilling to halt even for rest.

A knock at the door. Elizabeth.

"Come in," I said.

A dreamy, ecstatic look on her face. Fading instantly

when she saw the two of us entangled on the bed. A questioning frown. "We've been mating," I explained. "Did you think I was a complete hermit?" She looked from Swanson to me, from me to Swanson. Hand over her mouth. Eyes anguished. I turned the screw a little tighter. "I couldn't stop you from falling in love with me, Elizabeth. But I really do prefer my own kind. As should have been obvious."

"To have her here now, though—when you knew I was coming back—"

"Not *her,* exactly. Not *him* exactly either, though."

"—so cruel, David! To ruin such a beautiful experience." Holding forth sheets of paper with shaking hands. "A whole sonnet cycle," she said. "About tonight. How beautiful it was, and all. And now—and now—" Crumpling the pages. Hurling them across the room. Turning. Running out, sobbing furiously. Hell hath no fury like. *"David!"* A smothered cry. And slamming the door.

* * *

She was back in ten minutes. Swanson and I hadn't quite finished donning our bodies yet; we were both still unsealed. As we worked, we discussed further steps to take: he felt honor demanded that I request a transfer back to Homeworld, having terminated my usefulness here through tonight's indiscreet revelation. I agreed with him to some degree but was reluctant to leave. Despite the bodily torment of life on Earth I had come to feel I belonged here. Then Elizabeth entered, radiant.

"I mustn't be so possessive," she announced. "So bourgeois. So conventional. I'm willing to share my love." Embracing Swanson. Embracing me. "A *ménage à trois,"* she said. "I won't mind that you two are having a physical relationship. As long as you don't shut me out of your lives completely. I mean, David, we could never have been physical anyway, right, but we can have the other aspects of love, and we'll open ourselves to your friend also. Yes? Yes? Yes?"

* * *

Swanson and I both put in applications for transfer, he to Africa, me to Homeworld. It would be some time before we received a reply. Until then we were at her mercy. He was blazingly angry with me for involving him in this, but what choice had I had? Nor could either of us avoid Elizabeth. We were at her mercy. She bathed both of us in shimmering waves of tender emotion; wherever we turned, there she was, incandescent with love. Lighting up the darkness of our lives. You poor lonely creatures. Do you suffer much in our gravity? What about the heat? And the winters. Is there a custom of marriage on your planet? Do you have poetry?

A happy threesome. We went to the theater together. To concerts. Even to parties in Greenwich Village. "My friends," Elizabeth said, leaving no doubt in anyone's mind that she was living with both of us. Faintly scandalous doings; she loved to seem daring. Swanson was sullenly obliging, putting up with her antics but privately haranguing me for subjecting him to all this. Elizabeth got out another mimeographed booklet of poems, dedicated to both of us. *Triple Tripping,* she called it. Flagrantly erotic. I quoted a few of the poems in one of my reports of Homeworld, then lost heart and hid the booklet in the closet. "Have you heard about your transfer yet?" I asked Swanson at least twice a week. He hadn't. Neither had I.

Autumn came. Elizabeth, burning her candle at both ends, looked gaunt and feverish. "I have never known such happiness," she announced frequently, one hand clasping Swanson, the other me. "I never think about the strangeness of you any more. I think of you only as people. Sweet, wonderful, lonely people. Here in the darkness of this horrid city." And she once said, "What if everybody here is like you, and I'm the only one who's really human? But that's silly. You must be the only ones of your kind here. The advance scouts. Will your planet invade ours? I do hope so! Set everything to rights. The reign of love and reason at last!"

"How long will this go on?" Swanson muttered.

* * *

At the end of October his transfer came through. He left without saying goodbye to either of us and without leaving a forwarding address. Nairobi? Addis Ababa? Kinshasa?

* * *

I had grown accustomed to having him around to share the burden of Elizabeth. Now the full brunt of her affection fell on me. My work was suffering; I had no time to file my reports properly. And I lived in fear of her gossiping. What was she telling her Village friends? ("You know David? He's not really a man, you know. Actually inside him there's a kind of crab-thing from another solar system. But what does that matter? Love's a universal phenomenon. The truly loving person doesn't draw limits around the planet.") I longed for my release. To go home; to accept my punishment; to shed my false skin. To empty my mind of Elizabeth.

My reply came through the ultrawave on November 13. Application denied. I was to remain on Earth and continue my work as before. Transfers to Homeworld were granted only for reasons of health.

I debated sending a full account of my treason to Homeworld and thus bringing about my certain recall. But I hesitated, overwhelmed with despair. Dark brooding seized me. "Why so sad?" Elizabeth asked. What could I say? That my attempt at escaping from her had failed? "I love you," she said. "I've never felt so *real* before." Nuzzling against my cheek. Fingers knotted in my hair. A seductive whisper. "David, open yourself up again. Your chest, I mean. I want to see the inner you. To make sure I'm not frightened of it. Please? You've only let me see you once." And then, when I had: "May I kiss you, David?" I was appalled. But I let her. She was unafraid. Transfigured by happiness. She is a cosmic nuisance, but I fear I'm getting to like her.

Can I leave her? I wish Swanson had not vanished. I need advice.

* * *

Either I break with Elizabeth or I break with Homeworld. This is absurd. I find new chasms of despondency every day. I am unable to do my work. I have requested a transfer once again, without giving details. The first snow of the winter today.

* * *

Application denied.

* * *

"When I found you with Swanson," she said, "it was a terrible shock. An even bigger blow than when you first came out of your chest. I mean, it was startling to find out you weren't human, but it didn't hit me in any emotional way, it didn't threaten me. But then, to come back a few hours later and find you with one of your own kind, to know that you wanted to shut me out, that I had no place in your life—Only we worked it out, didn't we?" Kissing me. Tears of joy in her eyes. How did this happen? Where did it all begin? Existence was once so simple. I have tried to trace the chain of events that brought me from there to here, and I cannot. I was outside of my false body for eight hours today. The longest spell so far. Elizabeth is talking of going to the islands with me for the winter. A secluded cottage that her friends will make available. Of course, I must not leave my post without permission. And it takes months simply to get a reply.

* * *

Let me admit the truth: I love her.

* * *

January 1. The new year begins. I have sent my resignation to Homeworld and have destroyed my ultrawave equipment. The links are broken. Tomorrow, when the city offices are open, Elizabeth and I will go to get the marriage license.

Black Is Beautiful

my nose is flat my lips are thick my hair is frizzy my
skin is black
is beautiful
is black is beautiful
I am James Shabazz age seventeen born august 13
1983 I am black I am afro I am beautiful this machine
writes my words as I speak them and the machine is
black
is beautiful

* * *

Elijah Muhammad's *The Supreme Wisdom* says:
    Separation of the so-called Negroes from their slave-
masters' children is a MUST. It is the only SOLUTION
to our problem. It was the only solution, according to
the Bible, for Israel and the Egyptians, and it will prove
to be the only solution for America and her slaves,
whom she mockingly calls her citizens, without granting
her citizenship. We must keep this in our minds at all
times that we are actually being mocked.

* * *

Catlike, moving as a black panther would, James Shabazz stalked through the city. It was late summer, and the pumps were working hard, sucking the hot air out from under the Manhattan domes and squirting it into the suburbs. There had been a lot of grinding about that lately. Whitey out there complained that all that hot air was wilting his lawns and making his own pumps work too hard. Screw Whitey, thought James Shabazz pleasantly. Let his lawns wilt. Let him complain. Let him get black in the face with complaining. Do the mother some good.

Silently, pantherlike, down Fifth Avenue to 53rd, across to Park, down Park to 48th. Just looking around. A big boy, sweatshiny, black but not black enough to suit him. He wore a gaudy five-colored dashiki, beads from Mali, flowing white belled trousers, a neat goatee, a golden earring. In his left rear pocket: a beat-up copy of the new novel about Malcolm. In his right rear pocket: a cute little sonic blade.

Saturday afternoon and the air was quiet. None of the hopterbuses coming through the domes and dumping Whitey onto the rooftops. They stayed home today, the commuters, the palefaces. Saturday and Sunday, the city was black. Likewise all the other days of the week after four P.M. Run, Whitey, Run! See Whitey run! Why does Whitey run? Because he don't belong here no more.

Sorry, teach. I shouldn't talk like that no more, huh?

James Shabazz smiled. The identity card in his pocket called him James Lincoln, but when he walked alone through the city he spurned that name. The slavemaster name. His parents stuck with it, proud of it, telling him that no black should reject a name like Lincoln. The dumb geeps! What did they think, that great-great-grandpappy was owned by Honest Abe? Lincoln was a tag some belching hillbilly stuck on the family a hundred fifty years ago. If anyone asks me today, I'm James Shabazz. Black. Proud of it.

Black faces mirrored him on every street. Toward him came ten diplomats in tribal robes, not Afros but Africans, a bunch of Yorubas, Ibos, Baules, Mandingos, Ashantis, Senufos, Bakongos, Balubas, who knew what, the real thing, anyway, black as night, so black they looked purple. No slavemaster blood in them! James Shabazz smiled, nodded. Good afternoon, brothers. Nice day! They took no notice of him, but swept right on, their conversation unbroken. They were not speaking Swahili, which he would have recognized, but some other foreign language, maybe French. He wasn't sure. He scowled after them. Who they think they are, walking around a black man's city, upnosing people like that?

He studied his reflection for a while in the burnished window of a jewelry shop. Ground floor, Martin Luther King Building. Eighty stories of polished black marble. Black. Black man's money built that tower! Black man's sweat!

Overhead came the buzz of a hopter after all. No commuters today, so they had to be tourists. James Shabazz stared up at the beetle of a hopter crossing the dull translucent background of the distant dome. It landed on the penthouse hopter stage of the King Building. He crossed the street and tried to see the palefaces stepping out, but the angle was too steep. Even so, he bowed ceremoniously. Welcome, massa! Welcome to the black man's metropolis! Soul food for lunch? Real hot jazz on 125th? Dancing jigaboo girls stripping at the Apollo? Sightseeing tour of Bedford-Stuyvesant and Harlem?

Can't tell where Bedford-Stuyvesant ends and Harlem begins, can you? But you'll come looking anyway.

Like to cut your guts up, you honkie mothers.

*   *   *

Martin Luther King said in Montgomery, Alabama, instructing the bus desegregators:

If cursed, do not curse back. If pushed, do not push back. If struck, do not strike back, but evidence love and good will at all times.

*   *   *

He sat down for a while in Lumumba Park, back of the 42nd Street Library, to watch the girls go by. The new summer styles were something pretty special: Congo Revival, plenty of beads and metal coils, but not much clothing except a sprayon sarong around the middle. There was a lot of grumbling by the old people. But how could you tell a handsome Afro girl that she shouldn't show her beautiful black breasts in public? Did they cover the boobies in the Motherland? Not until the missionaries came. Christ can't stand a pair of bares. The white girls cover up because they don't got much up there. Or maybe to keep from getting sunburned.

He admired the parade of proud jiggling black globes. The girls smiled to themselves as they cut through the park. They all wore their hair puffed out tribal style, and some of them even with little bone doodads thrust through it. There was no reason to be afraid of looking too primitive any more. James Shabazz winked, and some of them winked back. A few of the girls kept eyes fixed rigidly ahead; plainly it was an ordeal for them to strip down this way. Most of them enjoyed it as much as the men did. The park was full of men enjoying the show. James

Shabazz wished they'd bring those honkie tourists here. He'd love a chance to operate on a few of them.

Gradually he became aware of a huge, fleshy, exceedingly black man with grizzled white hair, sitting across the way pretending to be reading his paper, but really stealing peeks at the cuties going by. James Shabazz recognized him: Powell 43X Nissim, Coordinating Chairman of the Afro-Muslim Popular Democratic Party of Greater New York. He was one of the biggest men in the city, politically—maybe even more important than Mayor Abdulrahman himself. He was also a good friend of the father of James Shabazz, who handled some of Powell 43X's legal work. Four or five times a year he came around to discuss some delicate point, and stayed far into the night, drinking pot after pot of black coffee and telling jokes in an uproarious bellow. Most of his jokes were antiblack; he could tell them like any Kluxer. James Shabazz looked on him as coarse, vulgar, seamy, out of date, an old-line pol. But yet you had to respect a man with that much power.

Powell 43X Nissim peered over the top of his *Amsterdam News,* saw him, let out a whoop, and yelled, "Hey, Jimmy Lincoln! What you doin' here?"

James Shabazz stood up and walked stiffly over. "Getting me some fresh air, sir."

"Been working at the library, huh? Studying hard? Gonna be the first nigger president, maybe?"

"No, sir. Just walkin' around on a Saturday."

"Ought to be in the library," Powell 43X said. "Read. Learn. That's how we got where we are. You think we took over this city because we a bunch of dumb niggers?" He let out a colossal laugh. "We *smart,* man!"

James Shabazz wanted to say, "We took over the city because Whitey ran out. He dumped it on us, is all. Didn't take no brains, just staying power."

Instead he said, "I got a little time to take it easy yet, sir. I don't go to college for another year."

"Columbia, huh?"

"You bet. Class of '05, that's me."

"You gonna fool with football when you get to college?"

"Thought I would."

"You listen to me," said Powell 43X. "Football's okay for high school. You get yourself into politics instead up there. Debating team. Malcolm X Society. Afro League. Smart boy like you, you got a career in government ahead of you if you play it right." He jerked his head to one side and indicated a girl striding by. "You get to be somebody, maybe you'll have a few of those to play with." He laughed. The girl was almost six feet tall, majestic, deep black, with great heavy swinging breasts and magnificent buttocks switching saucily from side to side beneath her sprayon wrap. Conscious that all eyes were on her, she crossed the park on the diagonal, heading for the Sixth Avenue side. Suddenly three whites appeared at the park entrance: weekend visitors, edgy, conspicuous. As the black girl went past them, one turned, gaping, his eyes following the trajectory of her outthrust nipples. He was a wiry redhead, maybe twenty years old, in town for a good time in boogieville, and you could see the hunger popping out all over him.

"Honkie mother," James Shabazz muttered. "Could use a blade you know where."

Powell 43X clucked his tongue. "Easy, there. Let him look! What it hurt you if he thinks she's worth lookin' at?"

"Don't belong here. No right to look. Why can't they stay where they belong?"

"Jimmy—"

"Honkies right in Times Square! Don't they know this here's our city?"

* * *

Marcus Garvey said:

*The Negro needs a Nation and a country of his own,
where he can best show evidence of his own ability in
the art of human progress. Scattered as an unmixed and
unrecognized part of alien nations and civilizations is
but to demonstrate his imbecility, and point him out as
an unworthy derelict, fit neither for the society of Greek,
Jew, or Gentile.*

* * *

While he talked with Powell 43X, James Shabazz kept
one eye on the honkie from the suburbs. The redhead
and his two pals cut out in the direction of 41st Street.
James Shabazz excused himself finally and drifted away,
toward that side of the park. Old windbag, he thought.
Nothing but a Tom underneath. Tolerance for the honkies! When did they tolerate *us?*

Easy, easy, like a panther. Walk slow and quiet.

Follow the stinking mother. Show him how it really is.

* * *

Malcolm X said:

*Always bear in mind that our being in the Western
hemisphere differs from anyone else, because everyone
else came here voluntarily. Everyone that you see in
this part of the world got on a boat and came here
voluntarily; whether they were immigrants or what have
you, they came here voluntarily. So they don't have any
real squawk, because they got what they were looking
for. But you and I can squawk because we didn't come
here voluntarily. We didn't ask to be brought here.
We were brought here forcibly, against our will, and in*

chains. And at no time since we have been here, have they even acted like they wanted us here. At no time. At no time have they ever tried to pretend that we were brought here to be citizens. Why, they don't even pretend. So why should we pretend?

* * *

The cities had been theirs for fifteen or twenty years. It had been a peaceful enough conquest. Each year there were fewer whites and more blacks, and the whites kept moving out, and the blacks kept getting born, and one day Harlem was as far south as 72nd Street, and Bedford-Stuyvesant had slopped over into Flatbush and Park Slope, and there was a black mayor and a black city council, and that was it. In New York the tipping point had come about 1986. There was a special problem there, because of the Puerto Ricans, who thought of themselves as a separate community; but they were outnumbered, and most of them finally decided it was cooler to have a city of their own. They took Yonkers, the way the Mexicans took San Diego. What it shuffled down to, in the end, was a city about eighty-five percent black and ten percent Puerto, with some isolated pockets of whites who stuck around out of stubborness or old age or masochism or feelings of togetherness with their black brothers. Outside the city were the black suburbs like Mount Vernon and Newark and New Rochelle, and beyond them, fifty, eighty, a hundred miles out, were the towns of the whites. It was apartheid in reverse.

The honkie commuters still came into the city, those who had to, quick-in quick-out, do your work and scram. There weren't many of them, really, a hundred thousand a day or so. The white ad agencies were gone north. The white magazines had relocated editorial staffs in the green suburbs. The white book publishers had followed the financial people out. Those who came in were corporate executives, presiding over all-black staffs; trophy whites, kept around by liberal-minded blacks for decoration; government employees, trapped by desegregation edicts; and odds and ends of other sorts, all out of place, all scared.

It was a black man's city. It was pretty much the same all across the country. Adjustments had been made.

* * *

Stokely Carmichael said:

We are oppressed as a group because we are black, not because we are lazy, not because we're apathetic, not because we're stupid, not because we smell, not because we eat watermelon and have good rhythm. We are oppressed because we are black, and in order to get out of that oppression, one must feel the group power that one has. . . . If there's going to be any integration it's going to be a two-way thing. If you believe in integration, you can come live in Watts. You can send your children to the ghetto schools. Let's talk about that. If you believe in integration, then we're going to start adopting us some white people to live in our neighborhood. . . .

. . . . We are not gonna wait for white people to sanction black power. We're tired of waiting.

* * *

South of 42nd Street things were pretty quiet on a Saturday, or any other time. Big tracts of the city were still empty. Some of the office buildings had been converted into apartment houses to catch the overflow, but a lot of them were still awaiting development. It took time for a black community to generate enough capital to run a big city, and though it was happening fast, it wasn't

happening fast enough to make use of all the facilities
the whites had abandoned. James Shabazz walked silently through silence, keeping his eyes on the three white
boys who strolled, seemingly aimlessly, a block ahead of
him.

He couldn't dig why more tourists didn't get cut up.
Hardly any of them did, except those who got drunk
and pawed some chick. The ones who minded their own
business were left alone, because the top men had
passed the word that the sightseers were okay, that they
injected cash into the city and shouldn't be molested. It
amazed James Shabazz that everybody listened. Up at
the Audubon, somebody would get up and read from
Stokely or Malcolm or one of the other black martyrs,
and call for a holy war on Whitey, really socking it to
'em. Civil rights! Equality! Black power! Retribution for
four hundred years of slavery! Break down the ghetto
walls! Keep the faith, baby! Tell it how it is! All about
the exploitation of the black man, the exclusion of the
Afros from the lily-white suburbs, the concentration of
economic power in Whitey's hands. And the audience
would shout amen and stomp its feet and sing hymns, but
nobody would ever do anything. *Nobody would ever do
anything*. He couldn't understand that. Were they satisfied to live in a city with an invisible wall around it? Did
they really think they had it so good? They talked about
owning New York, and maybe they did, but didn't they
know that it was all a fraud, that Whitey had given them
the damn city just so they'd stay out of *his* back yard?

Someday we gonna run things. Not the Powell 43X cats
and the other Toms, but *us*. And we gonna keep the city,
but we gonna take what's outside, too.

And none of this crap about honkie mothers coming in
to look our women over.

James Shabazz noted with satisfaction that the three
white boys were splitting up. Two of them were going
into Penn Station to grab the tube home, looked like. The
third was the redhead, and he was standing by himself

on Seventh Avenue, looking up at Uhuru Stadium, which he probably called Madison Square Garden. Good boy. Dumb enough to leave yourself alone. Now I gonna teach you a thing or two.

He moved forward quickly.

* * *

Robert F. Williams said:

When an oppressed people show a willingness to defend themselves, the enemy, who is a moral weakling and coward, is more willing to grant concessions and work for a respectable compromise.

* * *

He walked up smiling and said, "Hi, man. I'm Jimmy Lincoln."

Whitey looked perplexed. "Hi, man."

"You lookin' for some fun, I bet."

"Just came in to see the city a little."

"To find some fun. Lots of great chicks around here." Jimmy Lincoln winked broadly. "You can't kid me none. I go for 'em too. Where you from, Red?"

"Nyack."

"That's upstate somewhere, huh?"

"Not so far. Just over the bridge. Rockland County."

"Yeah. Nice up there, I bet. I never seen it."

"Not so different from down here. Buildings are smaller, that's all. Just as crowded."

"I bet they got a different-looking skin in Nyack," said Jimmy Lincoln. He laughed. "I bet I right, huh?"

The red-haired boy laughed too. "Well, I guess you are."

"Come on with me. I find you some fun. You and me. What's your name?"

"Tom."

"Tom. That's a good one. Lookee, Tom, I know a place, lots of girls, something to drink, a pill to pop, real soul music, yeah? Eh, man? Couple blocks from here. You came here to see the city, let me show it to you. Right?"

"Well—" uneasily.

"Don't be so up tight, man. You don't trust your black brother? Look, we got no feud with you. All that stuff's ancient history! You got to realize this is the year 2000, we all free men, we got what we after. Nobody gonna hurt you." Jimmy Lincoln moved closer and winked confidentially. "Lemme tell you something, too. That red hair of yours, the girls gonna orbit over that! They don't see that kind hair every day. Them freckles. Them blue eyes. Man, blue eyes, it turn them on! You in for the time of your life!"

Tom from Nyack grinned. He pointed toward Penn Station. "I came in with two pals. They went home, the geeps! Tomorrow they're going to feel awful dopey about that."

"You know they will," said Jimmy Lincoln.

They walked west, across Eighth Avenue, across Ninth, into the redevelopment area where the old warehouses had been ripped down. Signs sprouting from the acreage of rubble proclaimed that the Afro-American Cultural Center would shortly rise here. Just now the area looked bombed out. Tom from Nyack frowned as if he failed to see where a swinging nightclub was likely to be located in this district. Jimmy Lincoln led him up to 35th Street and around the hollow shell of a not quite demolished building.

"Almost there?" Tom asked.

"We here right now, man."

"Where?"

"Up against that wall, that's where," said James Shabazz. The sonic blade glided into his hand. He studded it and it began to whir menacingly. In a quiet voice he said, "Honkie, I saw you look at a black girl a little while ago like you might just be thinking about what's between her legs. You shouldn't think thoughts like that about black girls. You got an itch, man, you scratch it on your own kind. I think I'm gonna fix you so you don't itch no more."

* * *

Minister James 3X said:

> *First, there is fear—first and foremost there is inborn fear, and hatred for the black man. There is a feeling on the part of the white man of inferiority. He thinks within himself that the black man is the best man.*
> *The white man is justified in feeling that way because he has discovered that he is weaker than the black man. His mental power is less than that of the black man— he has only six ounces of brain and the Original Man has seven-and-a-half ounces. . . . The white man's physical power is one-third less than that of the black man.*

* * *

He had never talked this long with a honkie before. You didn't see all that many of them about, when you spent your time in high school. But now he stared into those frightened blue eyes and watched the blood drain from the scruffy white skin and he felt power welling up inside himself. He was Chaka Zulu and Malcolm and Stokely and Nkrumah and Nat Turner and Lumumba all rolled into one. He, James Shabazz, was going to lead the new black revolution, and he was going to begin by sacrificing this cowering honkie. Through his mind rolled the magnificent phrases of his prophets. He heard them talking, yes, Adam and Ras Tafari and Floyd, heard them singing down the ages out of Africa, kings in chains, martyrs, the great ones, he heard Elijah Muhammad and Muhammad Ali, Marcus Garvey, Sojourner Truth, du Bois, Henry Garnet, Rap Brown, rattling the chains, shouting for freedom, and all of them telling him, go on, man, how long you want to be a nigger anyhow? Go on! You think you got it so good? You gonna go to college, get a job, live in a house, eat steak and potatoes, and that's enough, eh, nigger, even if you can't set foot in Nyack, Peekskill, Wantagh, Suffern, Morristown? Be happy with what you got, darkie! You got more than we ever did, so why bitch about things? You got a city! You got power! You got freedom! It don't matter that they call you an ape. Don't matter that they don't let you near their daughters. Don't matter that you never seen Nyack. Be grateful for what you got, man, is that the idea?

He heard their cosmic laughter, the thunder of their derision.

And he moved toward Tom the honkie and said, "Here's where the revolution gets started again. Trash like you fooling with our women, you gonna get a blade in the balls. You go home to Nyack and give 'em that message, man."

Tom said lamely, "Look out behind you!"

James Shabazz laughed and began to thrust the blade home, but the anesthetic dart caught him in the middle of the back and his muscles surrendered, and the blade fell, and he turned as he folded up and saw the black policeman with the dart gun in his black fist, and he realized that he had known all along that this was how it would turn out, and he couldn't say he really cared.

* * *

Robert Moses of SNCC was questioned in May, 1962 on the voter registration drive in Mississippi:

Q: *Mr. Moses, did you know a person named Herbert Lee?*

A.: *Yes, he was a Negro farmer who lived near Liberty.*

Q: *Would you tell the Committee what Mr. Lee was doing and what happened?*

A: *He was killed on September 25th. That morning I was in McComb. The Negro doctor came by the voter registration office to tell us he had just taken a bullet out of a Negro's head. We went over to see who it was because I thought it was somebody in the voting program, and were able to identify the man as Mr. Herbert Lee, who had attended our classes and driven us around the voting area, visiting other farmers.*

* * *

Powell 43X Nissim said heavily, folding his hands across his paunch, "I got you off because you're your daddy's son. But you try a fool thing like that again, I gon' let them put you away."

James Shabazz said nothing.

"What you think you was doing, anyway, Jimmy? You know we watch all the tourists. We can't afford to let them get cut up. There was tracers on that kid all the time."

"I didn't know."

"You sit there mad as hell, thinking I should have let you cut him. You know who you really would have cut?

Jimmy Lincoln, that's who. We still got jails. Black judges know the law too. You get ruined for life, a thing like that. And what for?"

"To show the honkie a thing or two."

"Jimmy, Jimmy, Jimmy! What's to show? We got the whole city!"

"Why can't we live outside?"

"Because we don't *want* to. Those of us who can afford it, even, we stay here. They got laws against discrimination in this country. We stay here because we like it with our own kind. Even the black millionaires, and don't think there ain't plenty of 'em. We got a dozen men, they could *buy* Nyack. They stay."

"And why do you stay?"

"I'm in politics," said Powell 43X. "You know what a power base means? I got to stay where my people are. I don't care about living with the whites."

"You talk like you aren't even sore about it," James Shabazz said. "Don't you hate Whitey?"

"No. I don't hate no one."

"We all hate Whitey!"

"Only you hate Whitey," said Powell 43X. "And that's because you don't know nothin' yet. The time of hating's over, Jimmy. We got to be practical. You know, we got ourselves a good deal now, and we ain't gon' get more by burning nobody. Well, maybe the Stock Exchange moved to Connecticut, and a lot of banks and stuff like that, but *we run the city*. Black men. Black men hold the mortgages. We got a black upper crust here now. Fancy shops for black folk, fancy restaurants, black banks, gorgeous mosques. Nobody oppressing us now. When a mortgage gets foreclosed these days, it a *black* man doin' the foreclosin'. Black men ownin' the sweatshops. Ownin' the hockshops. Good and bad, we got the city, Jimmy. And maybe this is the way it meant to be: us in the cities, them outside."

"You talk like a Tom!"

"And you talk like a fool." Powell 43X chuckled.

"Jimmy, wake up! We all Toms today. We don't do revolutions now."

"I go to the Audubon," James Shabazz said. "I listen to them speak. They talk revolution there. They don't sound like no Toms to me!"

"It's all politics, son. Talk big, yell for equality. It don't make sense to let a good revolution die. They do it for show. A man don't get anywhere politickin' in black New York by sayin' that everything's one hundred percent all right in the world. And you took all that noise seriously? You didn't know that they just shoutin' because it's part of the routine? You went out to spear you a honkie? I figured you for smarter than that. Look, you all mixed up, boy. A smart man, black or white, he don't mess up a good deal for himself, even if he sometimes say he *want* to change everything all around. You full of hate, full of dreams. When you grow up, you'll understand. Our problem, it's not how to get out into the suburbs, it's how to keep Whitey from wanting to come back and live in here! We got to keep what we got. We got it pretty good. Who oppressing you, Jimmy? You a slave? Wake up! And now you understand the system a little better, clear your rear end outa my office. I got to phone up the mayor and have a little talk."

Jimmy Lincoln stumbled out, stunned, shaken. His eyes felt hot and his tongue was dry. The system? The *system?* How cynical could you get? The whole revolution phony? All done for show?

No. No. No. No.

He wanted to smash down the King Building with his fists. He wanted to see buildings ablaze, as in the old days when the black man was still fighting for what ought to be his.

I don't believe it, he thought. Not any of it. I'm not gonna stop fighting for my rights. I'm gonna live to see us overcome. I won't sell out like the others. Not me!

And then he thought maybe he was being a little dumb. Maybe Powell 43X was right: there wasn't anything left worth fighting for, and only a dopey kid would take the slogans at face value. He tried to brush that thought out of his head. If Powell 43X was right, everything he had read was a lot of crap. Stokely. Malcolm. All the great martyrs. Just so much ancient history?

He stepped out into the summer haze. Overhead, a hopterbus was heading for the suburbs. He shook his fist at it; and instantly he felt foolish for the gesture, and wondered why he felt foolish. And knew. And beneath his rebellious fury, began to suspect that one day he'd give in to the system too. But not yet. Not yet!

* * *

time to do my homework now

machine, spell everything right today's essay is on black power as a revolutionary force I am James Lincoln, Class 804, Frederick Douglass High School put that heading on the page yeah

the concept of black power as a revolutionary force first was heard during the time of oppression forty years ago, when

crap on that, machine, we better hold it until I know what I going to say

I am James Shabazz age seventeen born august 13 1983 I am black I am afro I am beautiful

black is beautiful

let's start over, machine

let's make an outline first

black power its origin its development the martyrdoms and lynchings the first black mayors the black congressmen and senators the black cities and then talk about black power as a continuing thing, the never-ending revolution no matter what pols like 43X say, never give in never settle for what they give you never sell out

that's it, machine
black power
black
black is beautiful

Ozymandías

The planet had been dead about a million years. That was our first impression, as our ship orbited down to its sere brown surface, and as it happened our first impression turned out to be right. There had been a civilization here *once*—but Earth had swung around Sol ten-to-the-sixth times since the last living being of this world had drawn breath.

"A dead planet," Colonel Mattern exclaimed bitterly. "Nothing here that's of any use. We might as well pack up and move on."

It was hardly surprising that Mattern would feel that way. In urging a quick departure and an immediate removal to some world of greater utilitarian value, Mattern was, after all, only serving the best interests of his employers. His employers were the General Staff of the Armed Forces of the United States of America. They expected Mattern and his half of the crew to produce results, and by way of results they meant new weapons and military alliances. They hadn't tossed in seventy percent of the budget for this trip just to sponsor a lot of archaeological putterings.

But luckily for *our* half of the outfit—the archaeological putterers' half—Mattern did not have an absolute voice in the affairs of the outfit. Perhaps the General Staff had kicked in for seventy percent of our budget, but the cautious men of the military's Public Liaison branch had seen to it that *we* had at least some rights.

Dr. Leopold, head of the nonmilitary segment of the expedition, said brusquely, "Sorry, Mattern, but I'll have to apply the limiting clause here."

Mattern started to sputter. "But—"

"But nothing, Mattern. We're here. We've spent a good chunk of American cash in getting here. I insist that we spend the minimum time allotted for scientific research, as long as we *are* here."

Mattern scowled, looking down at the table, supporting his chin on his thumbs and digging the rest of his fingers in hard back of his jawbone. He was annoyed, but he was smart enough to know he didn't have much of a case to make against Leopold.

The rest of us—four archaeologists and seven military men; they outnumbered us a trifle—watched eagerly as our superiors battled. My eyes strayed through the porthole and I looked at the dry windblown plain, marked here and there with the stumps of what might have been massive monuments millennia ago.

Mattern said bleakly, "The world is of utterly no strategic consequence. Why, it's so old that even the vestiges of civilization have turned to dust!"

"Nevertheless, I reserve the right granted to me to explore any world we land on, for a period of at least 168 hours," Leopold returned implacably.

Exasperated, Mattern burst out, "Dammit, *why?* Just to spite me? Just to prove the innate intellectual superiority of the scientist to the man of war?"

"Mattern, I'm not injecting personalities into this."

"I'd like to know what you *are* doing, then! Here we are on a world that's obviously useless to me and probably just as useless to you. Yet you stick me on a technicality and force me to waste a week here. Why, if not out of spite?"

"We've made only the most superficial reconnaissance so far," Leopold said. "For all we know this place may be the answer to many questions of galactic history. It may even be a treasure trove of superbombs, for all——"

"Pretty damned likely!" Mattern exploded. He glared around the conference room, fixing each of the scientific members of the committee with a baleful stare. He was making it quite clear that he was trapped into a wasteful expense of time by our foggy-eyed desire for Knowledge.

Useless knowledge. Not good hard practical knowledge of the kind *he* valued.

"All right," he said finally. "I've protested and I've lost, Leopold. You're within your rights in insisting on remaining here one week. But you'd damned well better be ready to blast off when your time's up!"

It had been foregone all along, of course. The charter of our expedition was explicit on the matter. We had been sent out to comb a stretch of worlds near the Galactic Rim that had already been brushed over hastily by a survey mission.

The surveyors had been looking simply for signs of life, and, finding none, they had moved on. We were entrusted with the task of investigating in detail. Some of the planets in the group had been inhabited once, the surveyors had reported. None bore present life.

Our job was to comb through the assigned worlds with diligence. Leopold, leading our group, had the task of doing pure archaeological research on the dead civilizations; Mattern and his men had the more immediately practical job of looking for fissionable material, leftover alien weapons, possible sources of lithium or tritium for fusion, and other militarily useful things. You could argue that in a strictly pragmatic sense our segment of the group was just dead weight, carted along for the ride at great expense, and you would be right.

But the public temper over the last few hundred years in America has frowned on purely military expeditions. And so, as a sop to the nation's conscience, five archaeologists, of little empirical consequence so far as national security mattered, were tacked onto the expedition.

Us.

Mattern made it quite clear at the outset that *his* boys were the Really Important members of the expedition, and that we were simply ballast. In a way, we had to agree. Tension was mounting once again on our sadly disunited planet; there was no telling when the Other Hemisphere would rouse from its quiescence of a hundred years and decide to plunge once more into space. If anything of military value lay out here, we knew we had to find it before They did.

The good old armaments race. Hi-ho! The old space stories used to talk about expeditions from Earth. Well, we *were* from Earth, abstractly speaking—but in actuality we were from America, period. Global unity was as much of a pipe dream as it had been three hundred years earlier, in the remote and primitive chemical-rocket era of space travel. Amen. End of sermon. We got to work.

The planet had no name, and we didn't give it one; a special commission of what was laughably termed the United Nations Organization was working on the problem of assigning names to the hundreds of worlds of the galaxy, using the old idea of borrowing from ancient Terran mythologies in analogy to the Mercury-Venus-Mars nomenclature of our own system.

Probably they would end up saddling this world with something like Thoth or Bel-Marduk or perhaps Avalo-kitesvara. We knew it simply as Planet Four of the system belonging to a yellow-white F5 IV Procyonoid sun, Revised HD Catalog 170861.

It was roughly Earthtype, with a diameter of 6100 miles, a gravity index of .93, a mean temperature of 45 degrees F. with a daily fluctuation range of about ten degrees, and a thin, nasty atmosphere composed mostly of carbon dioxide with wisps of helium and hydrogen and the barest smidgeon of oxygen. Quite possibly the air had been breathable by humanoid life millions of years ago—but that was—millions of years ago. We took good care to practice our breathing-mask drills before we ventured out of the ship.

The sun, as noted, was an F5 IV and fairly hot, but Planet Four was 185 million miles away from it at perihelion, and a good deal further when it was at the other swing of its rather eccentric orbit; the good old Keplerian ellipse took quite a bit of punishment in this system. Planet Four reminded me in many ways of Mars—except that Mars, of course, had never known intelligent life of any kind, at least none that had troubled to leave a hint of its existence, while this planet had obviously had a flourishing civilization at a time when Pithecanthropus was Earth's noblest being.

In any event, once we had thrashed out the matter of whether or not we were going to stay here or pull up and head for the next planet on our schedule, the five of us set to work. We knew we had only a week—Mattern would never grant us an extension unless we came up with something good enough to change his mind, which was improbable—and we wanted to get as much done in that week as possible. With the sky as full of worlds as it is, this planet might never be visited by Earth scientists again.

Mattern and his men served notice right away that they were going to help us, but reluctantly and minimally. We unlimbered the three small halftracks carried aboard ship and got them into functioning order. We stowed our gear —cameras, picks and shovels, camel's-hair brushes—and donned our breathing masks, and Mattern's men helped us get the halftracks out of the ship and pointed in the right direction.

Then they stood back and waited for us to shove off.

"Don't any of you plan to accompany us?" Leopold asked. The halftracks each held up to four men.

Mattern shook his head. "You fellows go out by yourselves today and let us know what you find. We can make better use of the time filing and catching up on back log entries."

I saw Leopold start to scowl. Mattern was being openly contemptuous; the least he could do was have his men make a token search for fissionable or fusionable matter! But Leopold swallowed down his anger.

"Okay," he said. "You do that. If we come across any raw veins of plutonium I'll radio back."

"Sure," Mattern said. "Thanks for the favor. Let me know if you find a brass mine, too." He laughed harshly. "Raw plutonium! I half believe you're serious!"

We had worked out a rough sketch of the area, and we split up into three units. Leopold, alone, headed straight due west, toward the dry riverbed we had spotted from the air. He intended to check alluvial deposits, I guess.

Marshall and Webster, sharing one halftrack, struck out to the hilly country southeast of our landing point. A substantial city appeared to be buried under the sand there. Gerhardt and I, in the other vehicle, made off to the north, where we hoped to find remnants of yet another city. It was a bleak, windy day; the endless sand that covered this world mounted into little dunes before us, and the wind picked up handfuls and tossed it against the plastite dome that covered our truck. Underneath the steel cleats of our tractor belt, there was a steady crunch-crunch of metal coming down on sand that hadn't been disturbed in millennia.

Neither of us spoke for a while. Then Gerhardt said, "I hope the ship's still there when we get back to the base."

Frowning, I turned to look at him as I drove. Gerhardt had always been an enigma: a small scrunchy guy with untidy brown hair flapping in his eyes, eyes that were set a little too close together. He had a degree from the University of Kansas and had put in some time on their field staff with distinction, or so his references said.

I said, "What the hell do you mean?"

"I don't trust Mattern. He hates us."

"He doesn't. Mattern's no villain—just a fellow who wants to do his job and go home. But what do you mean, the ship not being there?"

"He'll blast off without us. You see the way he sent us all out into the desert and kept his own men back. I tell you, he'll strand us here!"

I snorted. "Don't be a paranoid. Mattern won't do anything of the sort."

"He thinks we're dead weight on the expedition," Gerhardt insisted. "What better way to get rid of us?"

The halftrack breasted a hump in the desert. I kept wishing a vulture would squeal somewhere, but there was not even that. Life had left this world ages ago. I said, "Mattern doesn't have much use for *us,* sure. But would he blast off and leave three perfectly good halftracks behind? Would he?"

It was a good point. Gerhardt grunted agreement after a while. Mattern would *never* toss equipment away, though he might not have such scruples about five surplus archaeologists.

We rode along silently for a while longer. By now we had covered twenty miles through this utterly barren land. As far as I could see, we might just as well have stayed at the ship. At least there we had a surface lie of building foundations.

But another ten miles and we came across our city. It seemed to be of linear form, no more than half a mile wide and stretching out as far as we could see—maybe six or seven hundred miles; if we had time, we would check the dimensions from the air.

Of course it wasn't much of a city. The sand had pretty well covered everything, but we could see foundations jutting up here and there, weathered lumps of structural concrete and reinforced metal. We got out and unpacked the power shovel.

An hour later, we were sticky with sweat under our thin spacesuits and we had succeeded in transferring a few thousand cubic yards of soil from the ground to an area a dozen yards away. We had dug one devil of a big hole in the ground.

And we had nothing.

Nothing. Not an artifact, not a skull, not a yellowed tooth. No spoons, no knives, no baby rattles.

Nothing.

The foundations of some of the buildings had endured, though whittled down to stumps by a million years of sand and wind and rain. But nothing else of this civilization had survived. Mattern, in his scorn, had been right, I admitted ruefully: this planet was as useless to us as it was to them. Weathered foundations could tell us little except that there had once been a civilization here. An imaginative paleontologist can reconstruct a dinosaur from a fragment of a thighbone, can sketch out a presentable saurian with only a fossilized ischium to guide him. But could we extrapolate a culture, a code of laws, a technology, a philosophy, from bare weathered building foundations?

Not very likely.

We moved on and dug somewhere else half a mile away, hoping at least to unearth one tangible remnant of the civilization that had been. But time had done its work; we were lucky to have the building foundations. All else was gone.

"Boundless and bare, the lone and level sands stretch far away," I muttered.

Gerhardt looked up from his digging. "Eh? What's that?" he demanded.

"Shelley," I told him.

"Oh. Him."

He went back to digging.

Late in the afternoon we finally decided to call it quits and head back to the base. We had been in the field for seven hours and had nothing to show for it except a few hundred feet of tridim films of building foundations.

The sun was beginning to set; Planet Four had a thirty-five-hour day, and it was coming to its end. The sky, always somber, was darkening now. There was no moon. Planet Four had no satellites. It seemed a bit unfair; Three and Five of the system each had four moons, while around the massive gas giant that was Eight a cluster of thirteen moonlets whirled.

We wheeled round and headed back, taking an alternate route three miles east of the one we had used on the way out, in case we might spot something. It was a forlorn hope, though.

Six miles along our journey, the truck radio came to life. The dry, testy voice of Dr. Leopold reached us:

"Calling Trucks Two and Three. Two and Three, do you read me? Come in, Two and Three."

Gerhardt was driving. I reached across his knee to key in the response channel and said, "Anderson and Gerhardt in Number Three, sir. We read you."

A moment later, somewhat more faintly, came the sound of Number Two keying into the three-way channel, and I heard Marshall saying, "Marshall and Webster in Two, Dr. Leopold. Is something wrong?"

"I've found something," Leopold said.

From the way Marshall exclaimed *"Really!"* I knew that Truck Number Two had had no better luck than we. I said, "That makes one of us, then."

"You've had no luck, Anderson?"

"Not a scrap. Not a potsherd."

"How about you, Marshall?"

"Check. Scattered signs of a city, but nothing of archaeological value, sir."

I heard Leopold chuckle before he said, "Well, *I've* found something. It's a little too heavy for me to manage by myself. I want both outfits to come out here and take a look at it."

"What is it, sir?" Marshall and I asked simultaneously, in just about the same words.

But Leopold was fond of playing the Man of Mystery.

He said, "You'll see when you get here. Take down my coordinates and get a move on. I want to be back at the base by nightfall."

Shrugging, we changed course to head for Leopold's location. He was about seventeen miles southwest of us, it seemed. Marshall and Webster had an equally long trip to make; they were sharply southeast of Leopold's position.

The sky was fairly dark when we arrived at what Leopold had computed as his coordinates. The headlamps of the halftrack lit up the desert for nearly a mile, and at first there was no sign of anyone or anything. Then I spotted Leopold's halftrack parked off to the east, and from the south Gerhardt saw the lights of the third truck rolling toward us.

We reached Leopold at about the same time. He was not alone. There was an—object—with him.

"Greetings, gentlemen." He had a smug grin on his whiskery face. "I seem to have made a find."

He stepped back and, as if drawing an imaginary curtain, let us take a peek at his find. I frowned in surprise and puzzlement. Standing in the sand behind Leopold's halftrack was something that looked very much like a robot.

It was tall, seven feet or more, and vaguely humanoid; that is, it had arms extending from its shoulders, a head on those shoulders, and legs. The head was furnished with receptor plates where eyes, ears, and mouth would be on humans. There were no other openings. The robot's body was massive and squarish, with sloping shoulders, and its dark metal skin was pitted and corroded as by the workings of the elements over uncountable centuries.

It was buried up to its knees in sand. Leopold, still grinning smugly (and understandably proud of his find) said, "Say something to us, robot."

From the mouth receptors came a clanking sound, the gnashing of—what? Gears?—and a voice came forth, oddly high-pitched but audible. The words were alien and were spoken in a slippery singsong kind of inflection. I felt a chill go quivering down my back.

"It understands what you say?" Gerhardt questioned.

"I don't think so," Leopold said. "Not yet, anyway. But when I address it directly, it starts spouting. I think it's a kind of—well, guide to the ruins, so to speak. Built by the ancients to provide information to passersby; only it seems to have survived the ancients and their monuments as well."

I studied the thing. It *did* look incredibly old—and sturdy; it was so massively solid that it might indeed have outlasted every other vestige of civilization on this planet. It had stopped talking, now, and was simply staring ahead. Suddenly it wheeled ponderously on its base, swung an arm up to take in the landscape nearby, and started speaking again.

I could almost put the words in its mouth: "*—and over here we have the ruins of the Parthenon, chief temple of Athena on the Acropolis. Completed in the year 438 B.C. it was partially destroyed by an explosion in 1687 while in use as a powder magazine by the Turks—*"

"It *does* seem to be a sort of a guide," Webster remarked. "I get the definite feeling that we're being given an historical narration now, all about the wondrous monuments that must have been on this site once."

"If only we could understand what it's saying!" Marshall exclaimed.

"We can try to decipher the language somehow," Leopold said. "Anyway, it's a magnificent find, isn't it? And—"

I began to laugh suddenly. Leopold, offended, glared at me and said, "May I ask what's so funny, Dr. Anderson?"

"Ozymandias!" I said, when I had subsided a bit. "It's a natural! Ozymandias!"

"I'm afraid I don't—"

"Listen to him," I said. "It's as if he was built and put here for those who follow after, to explain to us the glories of the race that built the cities. Only the cities are gone, and the robot is still here! Doesn't he seem to be saying, *'Look on my works, ye Mighty, and despair'?*"

" *'Nothing beside remains.'* " Webster quoted. "It's apt. Builders and cities all gone, but the poor robot doesn't know it, and delivers his spiel nonetheless. Yes. We ought to call him Ozymandias!"

Gerhardt said, "What shall we do with it?"

"You say you couldn't budge it?" Webster asked Leopold.

"It weighs five or six hundred pounds. It can move of its own volition, but I couldn't move it myself."

"Maybe the five of us—" Webster suggested.

"No," Leopold said. An odd smile crossed his face. "We will leave it here."

"What?"

"Only temporarily," he added. "We'll save it—as a sort of surprise for Mattern. We'll spring it on him the final day, letting him think all along that this planet was worthless. He can rib us all he wants—but when it's time to go, we'll produce our prize!"

"You think it's safe to leave it out here?" Gerhardt asked.

"Nobody's going to steal it," Marshall said.

"And it won't melt in the rain," Webster added.

"But—suppose it walks away?" Gerhardt demanded. "It can do that, can't it?"

Leopold said, "Of course. But where would it go? It will remain where it is, I think. If it moves, we can always trace it with the radar. Back to the base, now; it grows late."

We climbed back into our halftracks. The robot, silent once again, planted knee-deep in the sand, outlined against the darkening sky, swiveled to face us and lifted one thick arm in a kind of salute.

"Remember," Leopold warned us as we left. "Not one word about this to Mattern!"

At the base that night, Colonel Mattern and his seven aides were remarkably curious about our day's activities. They tried to make it seem as if they were taking a sincere interest in our work, but it was perfectly obvious to us that they were simply goading us into telling them what they had anticipated—that we had found absolutely nothing. This was the response they got, since Leopold forbade mentioning Ozymandias. Aside from the robot, the truth was that we *had* found nothing, and when they learned of this they smiled knowingly, as if saying that had we listened to them in the first place we would all be back on Earth seven days earlier, with no loss.

The following morning after breakfast Mattern announced that he was sending out a squad to look for fissionable materials, unless we objected.

"We'll only need one of the halftracks," he said. "That leaves two for you. You don't mind, do you?"

"We can get along with two," Leopold replied a little sourly. "Just so you keep out of our territory."

"Which is?"

Instead of telling him, Leopold merely said, "We've adequately examined the area to the southeast of here, and found nothing of note. It won't matter to us if your geological equipment chews the place up."

Mattern nodded, eyeing Leopold curiously as if the obvious concealment of our place of operations had aroused suspicions. I wondered whether it was wise to conceal information from Mattern. Well, Leopold wanted to play his little game, I thought; and one way to keep Mattern from seeing Ozymandias was not to tell him where we would be working.

"I thought you said this planet was useless from your viewpoint, Colonel," I remarked.

Mattern stared at me. "I'm sure of it. But it would be idiotic of me not to have a look, wouldn't it—as long as we're spending the time here anyway?"

I had to admit that he was right. "Do you expect to find anything, though?"

He shrugged. "No fissionables, certainly. It's a safe bet that everything radioactive on *this* planet has long since decomposed. But there's always the possibility of lithium, you know."

"Or pure tritium," Leopold said acidly. Mattern merely laughed, and made no reply.

Half an hour later we were bound westward again to the point where we had left Ozymandias. Gerhardt, Webster, and I rode together in one halftrack, and Leopold and Marshall occupied the other. The third, with two of Mattern's men and the prospecting equipment, ventured off to the southeast toward the area Marshall and Webster had fruitlessly combed the day before.

Ozymandias was where we had left him, with the sun coming up behind him and glowing round his sides. I wondered how many sunrises he had seen. Billions, perhaps.

We parked the halftracks not far from the robot and approached, Webster filming him in the bright light of morning. A wind was whistling down from the north, kicking up eddies in the sand.

"Ozymandias have remain here," the robot said as we drew near.

In English.

For a moment we didn't realize what had happened, but what followed afterward was a five-man quadruple take. While we gabbled in confusion the robot said, "Ozymandias decipher the language somehow. Seem to be a sort of guide."

"Why—he's parroting fragments from our conversation yesterday," Marshall said.

"I don't think he's parroting," I said. "The words form coherent concepts. He's *talking* to us!"

"Built by the ancients to provide information to passersby," Ozymandias said.

"Ozymandias!" Leopold said. "Do you speak English?"

The response was a clicking noise, followed moments

later by, "Ozymandias understand. Not have words enough. Talk more."

The five of us trembled with common excitement. It was apparent now what had happened, and the happening was nothing short of incredible. Ozymandias had listened patiently to everything we had said the night before; then, after we had gone, he had applied his million-year-old mind to the problem of organizing our sounds into sense, and somehow had succeeded. Now it was merely a matter of feeding vocabulary to the creature and letting him assimilate the new words. We had a walking and talking Rosetta Stone!

Two hours flew by so rapidly we hardly noticed their passing. We tossed words at Ozymandias as fast as we could, defining them when possible to aid him in relating them to the others already engraved on his mind.

By the end of that time he could hold a passable conversation with us. He ripped his legs free of the sand that had bound them for centuries—and, serving the function for which he had been built millennia ago, he took us on a guided tour of the civilization that had been and had built him.

Ozymandias was a fabulous storehouse of archaeological data. We could mine him for years.

His people, he told us, had called themselves the Thaiquens (or so it sounded)—had lived and thrived for three hundred thousand local years, and in the declining days of their history had built him, as indestructible guide to their indestructible cities. But the cities had crumbled, and Ozymandias alone remained—bearing with him memories of what had been.

"This was the city of Durab. In its day it held eight million people. Where I stand now was the Temple of Decamon, sixteen hundred feet of your measurement high. It faced the Street of the Winds—"

"The Eleventh Dynasty was begun by the accession to the Presidium of Chonnigar IV, in the eighteen thousandth year of the city. It was in the reign of this dynasty that the neighboring planets first were reached—"

"The Library of Durab was on this spot. It boasted fourteen million volumes. None exist today. Long after the builders had gone, I spent time reading the books of the Library and they are memorized within me—"

"The Plague struck down nine thousand a day for more than a year, in that time—"

It went on and on, a cyclopean newsreel, growing in detail as Ozymandias absorbed our comments and added new words to his vocabulary. We followed the robot as he wheeled his way through the desert, our recorders gobbling in each word, our minds numbed and dazed by the magnitude of our find. In this single robot lay waiting to be tapped the totality of a culture that had lasted three hundred thousand years! We could mine Ozymandias the rest of our lives, and still not exhaust the fund of data implanted in his all-encompassing mind.

When, finally, we ripped ourselves away and, leaving Ozymandias in the desert, returned to the base, we were full to bursting. Never in the history of our science had such a find been vouchsafed: a complete record, accessible and translated for us.

We agreed to conceal our find from Mattern once again. But, like small boys newly given a toy of great value, we found it hard to hide our feelings. Although we said nothing explicit, our overexcited manner certainly must have hinted to Mattern that we had not had as fruitless a day as we had claimed.

That, and Leopold's refusal to tell him exactly where we had been working during the day, must have aroused Mattern's suspicions. In any event, during the night as we lay in bed I heard the sound of halftracks rumbling off into the desert; and the following morning, when we entered the mess hall for breakfast, Mattern and his men, unshaven and untidy, turned to look at us with peculiar vindictive gleams in their eyes.

Mattern said, "Good morning, gentlemen. We've been waiting for some time for you to arise."

"It's no later than usual, is it?" Leopold asked.

"Not at all. But my men and I have been up all night. We—ah—did a bit of archaeological prospecting while you slept." The colonel leaned forward, fingering his rumpled lapels, and said, "Dr. Leopold, for what reason did you choose to conceal from me the fact that you had discovered an object of extreme strategic importance?"

"What do you mean?" Leopold demanded—with a quiver taking the authority out of his voice.

"I mean," said Mattern quietly, "the robot you named Ozymandias. Just why did you decide not to tell me about it?"

"I had every intention of doing so before our departure," Leopold said.

Mattern shrugged. "Be that as it may. You concealed the existence of your find. But your manner last night led us to investigate the area—and since the detectors showed a metal object some twenty miles to the west, we headed that way. Ozymandias was quite surprised to learn that there were other Earthmen here."

There was a moment of crackling silence. Then Leopold said, "I'll have to ask you not to meddle with that robot, Colonel Mattern. I apologize for having neglected to tell you of it—I didn't think you were quite so interested in our work—but now I must insist you and your men keep away from it."

"Oh?" Mattern said crisply. "Why?"

"Because it's an archaeological treasure trove, Colonel. I can't begin to stress its value to us. Your men might perform some casual experiment with it and short-circuit its memory channels, or something like that. And so I'll have to assert the rights of the archaeological group of this expedition. I'll have to declare Ozymandias part of our preserve, and off bounds for you."

Mattern's voice suddenly hardened. "Sorry, Dr. Leopold. You can't invoke that now."

"Why not?"

"Because Ozymandias is part of *our* preserve. And off bounds for you, Doctor."

I thought Leopold would have an apoplectic fit right there in the mess hall. He stiffened and went white and strode awkwardly across the room toward Mattern. He choked out a question, inaudible to me.

Mattern replied, "Security, Doctor. Ozymandias is of military use. Accordingly we've brought him to the ship and placed him in sealed quarters, under top-level wraps. With the power entrusted to me for such emergencies, I'm declaring this expedition ended. We return to Earth at once with Ozymandias."

Leopold's eyes bugged. He looked at us for support, but we said nothing. Finally, incredulously, he said, "He's— of military use?"

"Of course. He's a storehouse of data on the ancient Thaiquen weapons. We've already learned things from him that are unbelievable in their scope. Why do you think this planet is bare of life, Dr. Leopold? Not even a blade of grass? A million years won't do that. But a superweapon *will*. The Thaiquens developed that weapon. And others, too. Weapons that can make your hair curl. And Ozymandias knows every detail of them. Do you think we can waste time letting you people fool with that robot, when he's loaded with military information that can make America totally impregnable? Sorry, Doctor. Ozymandias is your find, but he belongs to us. And we're taking him back to Earth."

Again the room was silent. Leopold looked at me, at Webster, at Marshall, at Gerhardt. There was nothing that could be said.

This was basically a militaristic mission. Sure, a few archaeologists had been tacked onto the crew, but fundamentally it was Mattern's men and not Leopold's who were important. We weren't out here so much to increase the fund of general knowledge as to find new weapons and new sources of strategic materials for possible use against the Other Hemisphere.

And new weapons had been found. New, undreamed-of weapons, product of a science that had endured for three hundred thousand years. All locked up in Ozymandias' imperishable skull.

In a harsh voice Leopold said, "Very well, Colonel. I can't stop you, I suppose."

He turned and shuffled out without touching his food, a broken, beaten, suddenly very old man.

I felt sick.

Mattern had insisted the planet was useless and that stopping here was a waste of time; Leopold had disagreed, and Leopold had turned out to be right. We had found something of great value.

We had found a machine that could spew forth new and awesome recipes for death. We held in our hands the sum and essence of the Thaiquen science—the science that had culminated in magnificent weapons, weapons so superb they had succeeded in destroying all life on this world. And now we had access to those weapons. Dead by their own hand, the Thaiquens had thoughtfully left us a heritage of death.

Gray-faced, I rose from the table and went to my cabin. I wasn't hungry now.

"We'll be blasting off in an hour," Mattern said behind me as I left. "Get your things in order."

I hardly heard him. I was thinking of the deadly cargo we carried, the robot so eager to disgorge its fund of data. I was thinking what would happen when our scientists back on Earth began learning from Ozymandias.

The works of the Thaiquens now were ours. I thought of the poet's lines: *"Look on my works, ye Mighty—and despair."*

Caliban

They have all changed their faces to a standard model. It is the latest thing, which should not be confused with the latest Thing. The latest Thing is me. The latest thing, the latest fad, the latest rage, is for them all to change their faces to a standard model. I have no idea how it is done but I think it is genetic, with the RNA, the DNA, the NDA. Only retroactive. They all come out with blond wavy hair and sparkling blue eyes. And long straight faces with sharp cheekbones. And notched chins and thin lips curling in ironic smiles. Even the black ones: thin lips, blue eyes, blond wavy hair. And pink skins. They all look alike now. The sweet Aryanized world. Our entire planet. Except me. Meee.

* * *

I am imperfect. I am blemished. I am unforgiving. I am the latest Thing.

* * *

Louisiana said, Would you like to copulate with me? You are so strange. You are so beautiful. Oh, how I desire you, strange being from a strange time. My orifices are yours.

It was a thoughtful offer. I considered it a while, thinking she might be trying to patronize me. At length I notified her of my acceptance. We went to a public copulatorium. Louisana is taller than I am and her hair is a torrent of spun gold. Her eyes are blue and her face is long and straight. I would say she is about twenty-three years old. In the copulatorium she dissolved her clothes and stood naked before me. She was wearing gold pubic hair that day and her belly was flat and taut. Her breasts were round and slightly elongated and the nipples were very small. Go on, she said, now you dissolve your clothes.

I said, I am afraid to because my body is ugly and you will mock me.

Your body is not ugly, she said. Your body is strange but it is not ugly.

My body is ugly, I insisted. My legs are short and they curve outward and my thighs have bulging muscles and I have black hairy hair all over me. Like an ape. And there is this hideous scar on my belly.

A scar?

Where they took out my appendix, I told her.

This aroused her beyond all probability. Her nipples stood up tall and her face became flushed.

Your appendix? Your appendix was removed?

Yes, I said, it was done when I was fourteen years old, and I have a loathsome red scar on my abdomen.

She asked, What year was it when you were fourteen?

I said, It was 1967, I think.

She laughed and clapped her hands and began to dance around the room. Her breasts bounced up and down but her long flowing silken hair soon covered them, leaving only the stubby pinkish nipples poking through like buttons. 1967! she cried. Fourteen! Your appendix was removed! 1967!

Then she turned to me and said, My grandfather was born in 1967, I think. How terribly ancient you are. My helix-father's father on the countermolecular side. I didn't realize you were so very ancient.

Ancient and ugly, I said.

Not ugly, only strange, she said.

Strange and ugly, I said. Strangely ugly.

We think you are beautiful, she said. Will you dissolve your clothes now? It would not be pleasing to me to copulate with you if you keep your clothes on.

There, I said, and boldly revealed myself. The bandy legs. The hairy chest. The scarred belly. The bulging shoulders. The short neck. She has seen my lopsided face, she can see my dismal body as well. If that is what she wants.

She threw herself upon me, gasping and making soft noises.

* * *

TABLE 2.   AMINO ACID SUBSTITUTIONS IN POLYPEPTIDE ANTIBIOTICS

ANTIBIOTIC FAMILY	AMINO ACID IN THE MAJOR COMPONENT	REPLACEMENT
Actinomycins	D-Valine	D-Alloisoleucine
	L-Proline	4-Hydroxy-L-proline
		4-Keto-L-proline
		Sarcosine
		Pipecolic acid
		Azetidine-2-carboxylic acid
Bacitracins	L-Valine	L-Isoleucine
Bottromycins	L-Proline	3-Methyl-L-proline
Gramicidin A	L-Leucine	L-Isoleucine

Ilamycins	N-Methyl-L-leucine	N-Methyl-L-formyl-norvaline
Polymyxins	D-Phenylalanine	D-Leucine
	L-Isoleucine	L-Leucine
Quinoxaline antibiotics	N-Methyl-L-valine	N-Methyl-L-isoleucine
Sporidesmolides	D-Valine	A-Alloisoleucine
Tyrocidine	L-Phenylalanine	L-Tryptophan
	D-Phenylalanine	D-Tryptophan
Vernamycin B	D-Alanine	D-Butyrine

* * *

What did Louisiana look like before the change came? Did she have dull stringy hair thick lips a hook nose bushy black eyebrows no chin foul breath one breast bigger than the other splay feet crooked teeth little dark hairs around her nipples a bulging navel too many dimples in her buttocks skinny thighs blue veins in her calves protruding ears? And then did they give her the homogenizing treatment and make her the golden creature she is today? How long did it take? What were the costs? Did the government subsidize the process? Were the large corporations involved? How were these matters handled in the socialist countries? Was there anyone who did not care to be changed? Perhaps Louisiana was born this way. Perhaps her beauty is natural. In any society there are always a few whose beauty is natural.

* * *

Dr. Habakkuk and Senator Mandragore spent a great deal of time questioning me in the Palazzo of Mirrors. They put a green plastic dome over my head so that everything I said would be recorded with the proper nuance and intensity. Speak to us, they said. We are fascinated by your antique accent. We are enthralled by your primitive odors. Do you realize that you are our sole representative of the nightmare out of which we have awakened? Tell us, said the Senator, tell us about your brutally competitive civilization. Describe in detail the fouling of the environment. Explain the nature of national rivalry. Compare and contrast methods of political discourse in the Soviet Union and in the United States. Let us have your analysis of the sociological implications of the first voyage to the moon. Would you like to see the moon? Can we offer you any psychedelic drugs? Did you find Louisiana sexually satisfying? We are so glad to have you here. We regard you as a unique spiritual treasure. Speak to us of yesterday's yesterdays, while we listen entranced and enraptured.

* * *

Louisiana says that she is eighty-seven years old. Am I to believe this? There is about her a springtime freshness. No, she maintains, I am eighty-seven years old. I was born on March-alternate 11, 2022. Does that depress you? Is my great age frightening to you? See how tight my skin is. See how my teeth gleam. Why are you so disturbed? I am, after all, much younger than you.

* * *

TABLE XIX

Some Less Likely but Important Possibilities

1. "True" artificial intelligence
2. Practical use of sustained fusion to produce neutrons and/or energy

3. Artificial growth of new limbs and organs (either *in situ* or for later transplantation)

4. Room temperature superconductors

5. Major use of rockets for commercial or private transportation (either terrestrial or extraterrestrial)

6. Effective chemical or biological treatment for most mental illnesses

7. Almost complete control of marginal changes in heredity

8. Suspended animation (for years or centuries)

9. Practical materials with nearly "theoretical limit" strength

10. Conversion of mammals (humans?) to fluid breathers

11. Direct input into human memory banks

12. Direct augmentation of human mental capacity by the mechanical or electrical interconnection of the brain with a computer

13. Major rejuvenation and/or significant extension of vigor and life span—say 100 to 150 years

14. Chemical or biological control of character or intelligence

15. Automated highways

16. Extensive use of moving sidewalks for local transportation

17. Substantial manned lunar or planetary installations

18. Electric power available for less than .3 mill per kilowatt-hour

19. Verification of some extrasensory phenomena

20. Planetary engineering

21. Modification of the solar system

22. Practical laboratory conception and nurturing of animal (human?) foetuses

23. Production of a drug equivalent to Huxley's soma

24. A technological equivalent of telepathy

25. Some direct control of individual thought processes

* * *

I understand that in some cases making the great change involved elaborate surgery. Cornea transplants and cosmetic adjustment of the facial structure. A great deal of organ-swapping went on. There is not much permanence among these people. They are forever exchanging segments of themselves for new and improved segments. I am told that among some advanced groups the use of mechanical limb-interfaces has come to be common, in order that new arms and legs may be plugged in with a minimum of trouble. This is truly an astonishing era. Even so, their women seem to copulate in the old ways: knees up thighs apart, lying on right side left leg flexed, back to the man and knees slightly bent, etc., etc., etc. One might think they would have invented something new by this time. But perhaps the possibilities for innovation in the sphere of erotics are not extensive. Can I suggest anything? What if the woman unplugs both arms and both legs and presents her mere torso to the man? Helpless! Vulnerable! Quintessentially feminine! I will discuss it with Louisiana. But it would be just my luck that her arms and legs don't come off.

* * *

On the first para-Wednesday of every month Lieutenant Hotchkiss gives me lessons in fluid-breathing. We go to one of the deepest sub-levels of the Extravagance Building, where there is a special hyperoxygenated pool, for the use of beginners only, circular in shape and not at all deep. The water sparkles like opal. Usually the pool is crowded with children but Lieutenant Hotchkiss arranges for me to have private instruction since I am shy about revealing my body. Each lesson is much like the one before. Lieutenant Hotchkiss descends the gentle ramp that leads one into the pool. He is taller than I am and his hair is golden and his eyes are blue. Sometimes I have difficulties distinguishing him from Dr. Habakkuk and Senator Mandragore. In a casual moment the lieutenant confided that he is ninety-eight years old and therefore not really a contemporary of Louisiana's, although Louisiana has hinted that on several occasions in the past she has allowed the lieutenant to fertilize her ova. I doubt this inasmuch as reproduction is quite uncommon in this era and what probability is there that she would have permitted him to do it more than once? I think she believes that by telling me such things she will stimulate emotions of jealousy in me, since she knows that the primitive ancients were frequently jealous. Regardless of all this Lieutenant Hotchkiss proceeds to enter the water. It reaches his navel, his broad hairless chest, his throat, his chin, his sensitive thin-walled nostrils. He submerges and crawls about on the floor of the pool. I see his golden hair glittering through the opal water. He remains totally submerged for eight or twelve minutes, now and again lifting his hands above the surface and waggling them as if to show me where he is. Then he comes forth. Water streams from his nostrils but he is not in the least out of breath. Come on, now, he says. You can do it. It's as easy as it looks. He beckons me toward the ramp. Any child can do it, the lieutenant assures me. It's a matter of control and determination. I shake my head. No, I say, genetic modification has something to do with it. My lungs aren't equipped to handle water, although I suppose yours are. The lieutenant merely laughs.

Come on, come on, into the water. And I go down the ramp. How the water glows and shimmers! It reaches my navel, my black-matted chest, my throat, my chin, my wide thick nostrils. I breathe it in and choke and splutter; and I rush up the ramp, struggling for air. With the water a leaden weight in my lungs. I throw myself exhausted to the marble floor and cry out, No, no, no, it's impossible. Lieutenant Hotchkiss stands over me. His body is without flaw. He says, You've got to try to cultivate the proper attitudes. Your mental set determines everything. Let's think more positively about this business of breathing under water. Don't you realize that it's a major evolutionary step, one of the grand and glorious things separating our species from the australopithecines? Don't you want to be part of the great leap forward? Up, now. Try again. Thinking positively all the time. Carrying in your mind the distinction between yourself and our bestial ancestors. Go in. In. In. And I go in. And moments later burst from the water, choking and spluttering. This takes place on the first para-Wednesday of every month. The same thing, every time.

* * *

When you are talking on the telephone and your call is abruptly cut off, do you worry that the person on the other end will think you have hung up on him? Do you suspect that the person on the other end has hung up on you? Such problems are unknown here. These people make very few telephone calls. We are beyond mere communication in this era, Louisiana sometimes remarks.

* * *

Through my eyes these people behold their shining plastic epoch in proper historical perspective. They must see it as the present, which is always the same. But to me it is the future and so I have the true observer's parallax: I can say, it once was like *that* and now it is like *this*. They prize my gift. They treasure me. People come from other continents to run their fingers over my face. They tell me how much they admire my asymmetry. And they ask me many questions. Most of them ask about their own era rather than about mine. Such questions as:

Does suspended animation tempt you?

Was the fusion plant overwhelming in its implications of contained might?

Can you properly describe interconnection of the brain with a computer as an ecstatic experience?

Do you approve of modification of the solar system?

And also there are those who make more searching demands on my critical powers, such as Dr. Habakkuk and Senator Mandragore. They ask such questions as:

Was the brevity of your life span a hindrance to the development of the moral instincts?

Do you find our standardization of appearance at all abhorrent?

What was your typical emotional response to the sight of the dung of some wild animal in the streets?

Can you quantify the intensity of your feelings concerning the transience of human institutions?

I do my best to serve their needs. Often it is a strain to answer them in meaningful ways, but I strive to do so. Wondering occasionally if it would not have been more valuable for them to interrogate a Neanderthal. Or one of Lieutenant Hotchkiss' australopithecines. I am perhaps not primitive enough, though I do have my own charisma, nevertheless.

* * *

Members of the new animal phylum, Gnathostomulida, recently discovered in Europe, have now been found in unexpected abundance and diversity along the east coast of the United States.

Two million animal species have been described, but the rate at which new descriptions accumulate indicates that these two million are only about fifty percent of the extant species on earth. The increase in new species of birds (8600 known species) has sunk to less than 0.3 percent a year, but in many other classes (for example, Turbellaria with 2500 known species) the rate of increase indicates that undescribed species probably total more than eighty percent. Although only about half of the existing kinds of animals have been described, eighty percent of the families, ninety-five percent of the orders, and nearly all of the animal classes are presumably already known. Therefore a new phylum should be rare indeed.

* * *

The first day it was pretty frightening for me. I saw one of them, with his sleek face and all, and I could accept that, but then another one came into the room to give me an injection, and he looked just like the first one. Twins, I thought, my doctors are twins. But then a third and a fourth and a fifth arrived. The same face, the very same fucking face. Imagine my chagrin, me with my blob of a nose, with my uneven teeth, with my eyebrows that meet in the middle, with my fleshy pockmarked cheeks, lying there beneath this convocation of the perfect. Let me tell you I felt out of place. I was never touchy about my looks before—I mean, it's an imperfect world, we all have our flaws—but these bastards *didn't* have flaws, and that was a hard acceptance for me to relate to. I thought I was being clever: I said, You're all multiples of the same gene pattern, right? Modern advances in medicine have made possible an infinite reduplication of genetic information and the five of you belong to one clone, isn't that it? And several of them answered, No, this is not the case, we are in fact wholly unrelated but within the last meta-week we have independently decided to standardize our appearance according to the presently favored model. And then three or four more of them came into my room to get a look at me.

* * *

In the beginning I kept telling myself: *In the country of the beautiful the ugly man is king.*

* * *

Louisiana was the first one with whom I had a sexual liaison. We often went to public copulatoria. She was easy to arouse and quite passionate although her friend Calpurnia informed me some months later that Louisiana takes orgasm-inducing drugs before copulating with me. I asked Calpurnia why and she became embarrassed. Dismayed, I bared my body to her and threw myself on top of her. Yes, she cried, rape me, violate me! Calpurnia's vigorous spasms astonished me. The following morning Louisiana asked me if I had noticed Calpurnia swallowing a small purple spansule prior to our intercourse. Calpurnia's face is identical to Louisiana's but her breasts are farther apart. I have also had sexual relations with Helena, Amniota, Drusilla, Florinda, and Vibrissa. Before each episode of copulation I ask them their names so that there will be no mistakes.

* * *

At twilight they programmed an hour of red and green rainfall and I queried Senator Mandragore about the means by which I had been brought to this era. Was it by bodily transportation through time? That is, the physical lifting of my very self out of *then* and into *now*? Or was my body dead and kept on deposit in a freezer vault until these people resuscitated and refurbished it? Am I, perhaps, a total genetic reconstruct fashioned from a few fragments of ancient somatic tissue found in a baroque urn? Possibly I am only a simulated and stylized interpretation of twentieth-century man produced by a computer under intelligent and sympathetic guidance. How was it done, Senator? How was it done? The rain ceased. Leaving elegant puddles of blurred hue in the puddle-places.

* * *

Walking with Louisiana on my arm down Venus Avenue I imagined that I saw another man with a face like mine. It was the merest flash: a dark visage, thick heavy brows, stubble on the cheeks, the head thrust belligerently forward between the massive shoulders. But he was gone, turning a sudden corner, before I could get a good look. Louisiana suggested I was overindulging in hallucinogens. We went to an underwater theater and she swam below me like a golden fish, revolving lights glinting off the upturned globes of her rump.

* * *

This is a demonstration of augmented mental capacity said Vibrissa I wish to show you what the extent of human potentiality can be. Read me any passage of Shakespeare of your own choice and I will repeat it verbatim and then offer you textual analysis. Shall we try this? Very well I said and delicately put my fingernail to the Shakespeare cube and the words formed and I said out loud, What man dare, I dare: Approach thou like the rugged Russian bear, the arm'd rhinoceros, or the Hyrcan tiger, Take any shape but that, and my firm nerves Shall never tremble. Vibrissa instantly recited the lines to me without error and interpreted them in terms of the poet's penis-envy, offering me footnotes from Seneca and Strindberg. I was quite impressed. But then I was never what you might call an intellectual.

*   *   *

On the day of the snow-gliding events I distinctly and beyond any possibilities of ambiguity or misapprehension saw two separate individuals who resembled me. Are they importing more of my kind for their amusement? If they are I will be resentful. I cherish my unique status.

*   *   *

I told Dr. Habakkuk that I wished to apply for transformation to the facial norm of society. Do it, I said, the transplant thing or the genetic manipulation or however you manage it. I want to be golden-haired and have blue eyes and regular features. I want to look like you. Dr. Habakkuk smiled genially and shook his youthful golden head. No, he told me. Forgive us, but we like you as you are.

* * *

Sometimes I dream of my life as it was in the former days. I think of automobiles and pastrami and tax returns and marigolds and pimples and mortgages and the gross national product. Also I indulge in recollections of my childhood my parents my wife my dentist my younger daughter my desk my toothbrush my dog my umbrella my favorite brand of beer my wristwatch my answering service my neighbors my phonograph my ocarina. All of these things are gone. Grinding my flesh against that of Drusilla in the copulatorium I wonder if she could be one of my descendants. I must have descendants somewhere in this civilization, and why not she? She asks me to perform an act of oral perversion with her and I explain that I couldn't possibly engage in such stuff with my own great-grandchild.

* * *

I think I remain quite calm at most times considering the extraordinary nature of the stress that this experience has imposed on me. I am still self-conscious about my appearance but I pretend otherwise. Often I go naked just as they do. If they dislike bodily hair or disproportionate limbs, let them look away.

* * *

Occasionally I belch or scratch under my arms or do other primitive things to remind them that I am the authentic man from antiquity. For now there can be no doubt that I have my imitators. There are at least five. Calpurnia denies this but I am no fool.

* * *

Dr. Habakkuk revealed that he was going to take a holiday in the Carpathians and would not return until the 14th of June-surrogate. In the meantime Dr. Clasp would minister to my needs. Dr. Clasp entered my suite and I remarked on his startling resemblance to Dr. Habakkuk. He asked, What would you like? and I told him I wanted him to operate on me so that I looked like everybody else. I am tired of appearing bestial and primordial, I said. To my surprise Dr. Clasp smiled warmly and told me that he'd arrange for the transformation at once, since it violated his principles to allow any organism needlessly to suffer. I was taken to the operating room and given a sour-tasting anesthetic. Seemingly without the passing of time I awakened and was wheeled into a dome of mirrors to behold myself. Even as I had requested they had redone me into one of them, blond-haired, blue-eyed, with a slim agile body and a splendidly symmetrical face. Dr. Clasp came in after a while and we stood side by side: we might have been twins. How do you like it? he asked. Tears brimmed in my eyes and I said that this was the most wonderful moment of my life. Dr. Clasp pummeled my shoulder jovially and said, You know, I am not Dr. Clasp at all, I am really Dr. Habakkuk and I never went to the Carpathians. This entire episode has been a facet of our analysis of your pattern of responses.

* * *

Louisiana was astonished by my changed appearance. Are you truly he? she kept asking Are you truly he? I'll prove it I said and mounted her with my old prehistoric zeal, snorting and gnawing her breasts. But she shook me free with a deft flip of her pelvis and rushed from the chamber. You'll never see me again she shouted but I merely shrugged and called after her, So what I can see lots of others just like you. I never saw her again.

* * *

TABLE I
Composition of isocaloric diet

Substance	Composition (%)
Barley meal	70.0
Fine Millars Offal	20.0
Extracted soya bean meal	7.5
Salt	0.5
Ground limestone	0.5
Sterilized bone meal	1.0
"Eves" No. 32 (totally digestible)	0.25

* * *

Plausible attitudes upon discovering that one has been ripped from one's proper cultural matrix:

a) Fear

b) Indignation

c) Incredulity

d) Uncertainty

e) Aggressive hostility

f) Withdrawal

g) Compulsive masturbation

h) Cool acceptance

i) Suspicion

j) None of these

*   *   *

So now they have all changed themselves again to the new standard model. It happened gradually over a period of months but the transition is at last complete. Their heavy brows, their pockmarked cheeks, their hairy chests. It is the latest thing. I make my way through the crowded streets and wherever I turn I see faces that mirror my own lopsidedness. Only I am not lopsided myself any more, of course. I am symmetrical and flawless, and I am the only one. I cannot find Dr. Habakkuk and Dr. Clasp is in the Pyrenees; Senator Mandragore was defeated in the primary. So I must remain beautiful. Walking among them. They are all alike. Thick lips uneven teeth noses like blobs. How I despise them! I the only golden one. And all of them mocking me by their metamorphosis. All of them. Mocking me. Meee.

The Shrines of Earth

Master-poet Jorun Kedrik looked up at the nearly flawless blue sky and said, "Earth's a lovely world. It would be a pity if the Hrossai conquered it, wouldn't it?"

He was lying on a greenswarded, gently sloping hill just outside his current dwelling near ancient Paris. Earth no longer had cities, and nothing remained of old Paris, nothing but the one monstrosity of iron strutworks jutting nearly a thousand feet into the air half a mile away. Even at this distance, Kedrik's keen eyes picked out the bright robes of some tourists from New Gallia who were revisiting their ancestral shrine.

At his side, his companion, musician-apprentice Levri Amsler, was stretched face-down on the grass. Amsler, long-legged, angular-featured, said, "How certain is the invasion? When's it due?"

Kedrik shrugged. "Five years, six, maybe. Our best sociologists worked out the projection. The Hrossai will be coming down out of the Centauri system, and the first stop is Earth. It makes a convenient jumping-off point for their conquest of the galaxy."

"And they know they can knock us over without a fight," Amsler added mournfully. He rolled over, picked up his flute, and brushed a few strands of grass away from the mouthpiece. Pursing his lips, he played a brief, poignant melody, ending in a striking minor cadence.

"Nicely conceived," Kedrik said approvingly. "Perhaps the Hrossai will keep us alive as court musicians—you, at least." Then he chuckled harshly. "No, that's not likely. There's little place in their scheme of things for flute players or poets. They'll be looking for soldiers."

"They won't find any here," the younger man said, putting down the flute. "There isn't a man on Earth who'd know which end of a gun to point if a Hross gave it to him."

Kedrik rose and stretched. "Three thousand years of peace! Three thousand years of contentment! Well, it couldn't last forever, Levri. We were once the galaxy's fiercest fighters; if we want to survive the Hrossai onslaught, we'll have to relearn some of our ancient skills."

"No! Warfare, on Earth—again?" Amsler asked. "I'd almost think it would be better to let the Hrossai destroy us, you know?"

"Faulty thinking," Kedrik said testily. "Contrasurvival. Gutless. Foolish."

"What do you mean?"

"We were once the galaxy's most ruthless killers, when we needed to be," Kedrik said. "In the old days, we made the grubby little Hrossai look like saints." He grinned and added, "But we were also the galaxy's shrewdest intriguers. And *that's* a skill we haven't forgotten, I'd say?"

"What's on your mind, Jorun?"

"You'll see. Come: let's amble over to yonder ugly pile of metal and chat with those tourists from New Gallia. They always welcome a chance to gawk at the quaint pastoral types that inhabit their mother world."

New Gallia was a large, cheerful planet in the Albireo system. Lit by a double star, fifth-magnitude blue and third-magnitude yellow, the colony never lacked for sunlight of one color or another; the brighter yellow sun supplied most of the heat, the fifth-magnitude blue providing that extra touch of color, the decorative flair, that the New Gallians loved so dearly.

New Gallia had been the second extrasolar planet to be settled by Terran colonists, during the years of the great exodus. The *Jules Verne* had brought five hundred hand-picked couples there in 2316, ten years after the United States had planted its colony, Columbia, in the Sirius system, and five years before the *Boris Godunov* deposited its cargo of ex-Muscovites on the steppes of Novaya Ruthenia, formerly Procyon VI.

The current Chief of State on New Gallia was a slim, dark-complected mathematician named Justin LeFebvre, whose term of office, barring a collapse of the government, had still eight months to go. LeFebvre would have loved nothing more greatly than the overthrow of his government; he longed to rid himself of the tiresome job and return to Theory of Sets.

But duty was duty, and *someone* had to do the job. Furthermore, pride was pride. It was a point of honor for a New Gallian premier to survive in office for the duration of a full one-year term, and much as he hated the job, LeFebvre privately was doing his best not to lose it.

In his office on the seventy-second floor of the Bastille —named for some forgotten, legend-shrouded building of Earth—LeFebvre stared at the excited-looking man before him.

Frowning, the Chief of State said, "Slowly, my good man, slowly! Begin from the beginning, and tell me exactly what you heard, M. Dauzat."

M. Dauzat, a wealthy beet-farmer who had held the premiership a decade before, forced himself into a state of calm. "Very well, sir. As I said: my wife and I had decided at last to visit Earth, to see our ancestral world, the mother of our people. And, naturally, to pay our respects at the Tower."

"Naturally."

"We were, then, at the very base of the Tower, preparing to make the ascent, when a pair of natives approached us. Like all native Terrans, they were charming, simple people; they wore cloaks of gentle hues, carried musical instruments, and spoke in even more musical tones. Mme. Dauzat was quite taken with them."

"Of course," LeFebvre said impatiently. Now that he had slowed Dauzat down, there seemed to be no way of accelerating the pace of the narrative again. "We all know how charming the Terrans are. But go on."

"To be brief, we invited them to make the ascent of the Tower with us. We reached the top and gazed out over the peaceful green land that had once been France"—an expansive smile spread over Dauzat's heavy jowls—"and then the older of the two Terrans said, in a voice muffled with sadness, that it was indeed a misfortune that the uncultured savages from Columbia planned to destroy our noble Tower."

"What?"

LeFebvre paled; he rose stiffly from his webchair and stared in horror at Dauzat. "Would you say that again, M. Dauzat?"

"I only repeat what the native told me. He informed me that it was generally feared that Columbia intended to destroy the Tower, as the first step in a possible campaign planned at beginning open war between our worlds."

"I see," LeFebvre said numbly.

Relations between New Gallia and the American-settled planet Columbia had been, to say the least, strained, during the past four centuries—and only the existence of Novaya Ruthenia, the third major power in the galaxy, had kept the French and American colonies from war.

Right now, Novaya Ruthenia and New Gallia were enjoying uneasy "friendly relations," with each other, and both were on the outs with the Columbians. But in a war between New Gallia and Columbia, the Ruthenians would be sure to profit; the eager Russians would be quick to gobble up the best trade routes to such minor neutral worlds as Xanadu and Britannia.

But still, an attack on the Tower, the symbol and focal point of New Gallic life—! *Sacre bleu,* it was provocation for war!

Nodding to the fat man, LeFebvre said, *"Merci,* M. Dauzat. Your thoughtfulness in cutting short your vacation to return here with this disturbing news will not go unappreciated."

"I would have communicated with you direct," said Dauzat. "But the subradio channels are so uncertain, and I feared interception."

"You acted rightly, *M'sieu."* LeFebvre pushed the communicator stud on his desk and said, "An immediate Council meeting is called, top priority. Everyone is to be here. *Everyone."*

"The Radical ministers are holding a party caucus, M. LeFebvre," his secretary's emotionless voice informed him. "Shall I contact them?"

"By all means. Their caucus is of no importance now." Hoarsely he added, "Besides, they may be back in power by nightfall anyway. Only don't tell them that."

"Order, please, gentlemen. Order!"

LeFebvre pushed away the sheet of paper on which he had been calming himself with quadratics, and said once again, *"Order!"*

The room quieted. Seated to his left were seven ministers of his party, the Social Conservatives; to his right were the three Democratic Radical men he had chosen to include in his coalition government, plus four more Dem-Rads of high party standing but noncabinet status. He had invited them for the sake of equality; a crisis of this sort transcended mere party barriers.

"You've heard the story substantially as M. Dauzat gave it to me. Now, we all know and trust M. Dauzat— while those Terrans, of course, being inhabitants of France herself, were certainly telling the truth. Before we proceed, gentlemen, I'd like to call for a cabinet vote of confidence; I'll resign if it's your will."

The vote was seven for LeFebvre, three against. Le-Febvre remained in office.

"Now, then. We're faced with the prospect of an attack on the Eiffel Tower itself, as the opening move in a war Columbia is obviously planning to declare. Are there any suggestions?"

M. de Villefosse, Secretary of Interworld Affairs, leaned forward and said, "Certainly. We must arm ourselves at once, and prepare for this war!"

M. Raval, Secretary of Home Defense, said, "A good thought! We hold our ships in readiness, and strike at Columbia the instant the Tower is attacked. We could also, in retaliation, destroy the Columbians' own shrine on Earth."

"The Washington Monument?" said M. Bournon, Secretary of Culture. "But why wipe out two monuments? Why not simply establish a guard over our own?"

"The Terrans would not care for an armed enclave of our men on their territory," LeFebvre pointed out. "They might protest. They might enlist the aid of the Ruthenians, and then we'd face attack from both sides." The Premier's fingers trembled; he had never anticipated a crisis of this magnitude.

"I have the solution, then," announced M. de Simon, the Democratic-Radical Secretary of the Economy. "We establish a permanent guard force in space, in constant orbit around Earth. Our ships will remain forever on the lookout for this attack from Columbia, and will be ready to defend our Tower when the time comes."

"An excellent suggestion," said LeFebvre. "The Earthman won't object—I hope—and we won't be transgressing on anyone's national boundaries. We will, though, be able to defend the Tower. I call for a vote."

The vote was unanimous—the first time the New Gallian cabinet had so quickly agreed on anything in 384 years.

Deciding on the number of ships to be sent was a different matter. It took six hours, but at the end of that time it was officially determined that nine New Gallian ships of the line were to be sent to Earth as a defensive force, to protect New Gallia's most sacred shrine.

Premier LeFebvre slept soundly that night, dreaming of surds and integrals. The crisis was averted—or, at least, postponed. The government had not fallen. And, *le bon Dieu* grant it, Columbia would not decide to start its war for at least eight months, by which time LeFebvre would be a private citizen once again.

Pyotr Alexandrovitch Miaskovski, Acting Czar of all Novaya Ruthenia, squinted myopically at the slip of paper in his stubby fingers, and sighed.

It was a report from one of the Ruthenian scouts who patrolled the sector of the galaxy that included Sol. The despatch had just come in, over tight-beam subradio direct from the vicinity of Pluto. It said:

TO: Acting Czar Pyotr Alexandrovitch
FROM: Major-Colonel Ilya Ilyitch Tarantyev, First Scout Squadron.

Excellency:

A fleet of nine New Gallian vessels observed taking up orbits round Sol III. They seem armed. They appear to be preparing for large-scale military enterprise. Please advise.

Miaskovski fingered the despatch, made a sour face, and tapped his thumbs together unhappily. Somewhere, elsewhere in the royal palace, Czar Alexei lay peacefully sleeping, far removed from worldly cares.

Bozhe moi! Miaskovski thought dismally. The New Gallians were taking position around Earth? *Why?* Did this presage a war, a breaking down of the uneasy balance of power that had held between the three major worlds for so long?

And why did it have to happen now—now, when the

Czar lay wrapped in impenetrable catatonia and the cares of the state devolved upon *him?*

Miaskovski squared his shoulders. An election was scheduled for the following week, to choose the successor to Alexei. Miaskovski had been planning to run. He didn't intend to let a minor crisis like this upset his ambitions.

He flicked on the visiscreen, and the square-set, pudgy face of his secretary appeared.

"Olga, have the Ambassador from New Gallia sent here at once, will you?"

"Certainly, Excellency. At once."

Miaskovski broke the circuit and sat back in his heavy chair. *Uneasy lies the head,* he thought—but the Czarship was a coveted plum despite the headaches. His handling of this situation would help to sway the electorate next week, he hoped.

"You wish to see me, Czar Pyotr?"

He looked up. The lean face of Ambassador Selevine gleamed at him from the door vizor.

"Ah—yes. Come in, please, M. Selevine."

The door slid back and the New Gallian diplomat entered—dressed impeccably, as always. Pyotr felt a certain sense of inferiority; his thick, coarse garments appeared crude compared with the diplomatic costume the New Gallian affected.

The Acting Czar leaned back in his big chair, coughed, and said, "I'll be very blunt with you, M. Selevine. I want an explanation of this situation." He handed the New Gallian the scout's despatch.

"But of course, Your Majesty."

Selevine took the sheet and scanned it rapidly. Miaskovski watched closely; the diplomat appeared to be somewhat ruffled.

Selevine folded the paper neatly in half and placed it on the Czar's desk. He smiled coldly, revealing perfect white teeth.

"Nine ships," he remarked idly.

"Ahem—yes. Nine ships. Does your government have

any official explanation of this sudden entry into a neutral area?"

Selevine's smile vanished. "We do. The maneuver is strictly a defensive one, with no hostile intent whatever."

"Defensive? How so?"

"Be assured that the Free World of Novaya Ruthenia is not concerned in the matter, Czar Pyotr. It is strictly a matter between us and—and another planet, Your Majesty."

"Oh?" One of Pyotr's bushy eyebrows rose. "Would you care to expand on that theme, M. Selevine?"

The diplomat grinned frigidly. "One of my world's most revered shrines is located on Earth, Czar Pyotr. I refer, of course, to the Eiffel Tower. We—ah—have been given to understand that a rival power in the galaxy has designs against this shrine of ours, for motives that are not yet clear to us. We are merely taking precautions."

"You mean that the Columbians are planning to blast your damned tower?" Pyotr asked in surprise.

"I mentioned no world specifically, Excellency."

"Ah—of course."

The Acting Czar scratched his forehead for a moment, squinting surreptitiously at the New Gallian and trying without success to peer behind his diplomatic mask. "Very well, then," Pyotr said finally. "If I have your assurance that your world plans no hostile action against Novaya Ruthenia—"

"You have that assurance, Your Majesty."

"Then we can consider the matter no concern of Novaya Ruthenia's, or of mine. Good day, M. Selevine."

"Good day, Your Majesty. And kindly accept my best wishes for the forthcoming election."

"Ah—certainly. Thank you very much, M. Selevine."

When the diplomat had left, Miaskovski leaned back, frowning, and stared at the textured stucco of the ceiling, sorting out what he had learned.

Columbia planned an attack on the Eiffel Tower. The

New Gallians were establishing a defensive fleet to prevent that. Well, that made sense.

But Novaya Ruthenia had a shrine on earth too: the
heavy-walled Kremlin, relic of the long-forgotten empire
called Russia. Much as the Ruthenians wished to repudi-
ate their undemocratic past, they yet revered the massive
buildings of the Kremlin. What if the Columbians planned
an attack on that? Or suppose these New Gallian ships
had some such hidden idea? It wouldn't sit well with the
people—not at all. Assuming he were elected, his reign
as Czar would be brief.

Fight fire with fire, Miaskovski thought.

"I want to talk to the Commissar of Security," he
barked into the visiscreen.

And when the flat-featured face of Onegin, Commissar
of Security, appeared on the screen, Czar Pyotr said,
"Can you spare ten warships at once, Porfiry Mikheitch?"

The Commissar looked startled. "I—I suppose so,
Majesty. But—"

"Good. I want ten fully armed warships sent to the
Sol sector at once. They're to be placed in orbit around
Sol III—Earth—with an eye toward guarding against a
possible New Gallian or Columbian attack on the Kremlin. And make sure your commanders know that this is
strictly a defensive maneuver!"

"Certainly, Majesty," the Commissar said in a weak
voice. "I'll tend to it at once."

There was a hubbub in the office of James Edgerly,
President of the Republic of Columbia. Edgerly himself,
a tall, spare man in his early eighties, prematurely grayed
around the temples, stood at the center of the commotion,
while assorted members of his staff tried to make themselves heard over each others' shouts.

"Quiet!" Edgerly finally roared. *"Shut up!"*

That did it. The President glared belligerently around
the room and said, "All right. Let's hear those reports
one at a time. McMahon, you're first."

The Chief of Intelligence smiled dourly. "Yessir. As I think you may know, Mr. President, we picked up a subradio message from a Russian—I mean Ruthenian—scout last week. The message said the scout had discovered nine New Gallian ships in orbit around Earth. Later, a couple of Columbian tourists visiting ancient America confirmed this. They even saw one of the New Gallian ships circle the Washington Monument and disappear in the direction of the Atlantic."

"Fill me in on the Atlantic," President Edgerly ordered.

An aide named Goodman whose job this was immediately recited, "The Atlantic is the ocean separating the Eastern from the Western Hemispheres. America is at one side, and Europe on the other."

"Okay." Edgerly turned to Sheldrick, the Chief of Security. "Give me the scout report now, Sheldrick."

"Well, sir, as soon as we intercepted the message from that Ruthenian scout, I ordered a couple of our ships into the area to take a look. And sure enough, nine New Gallian ships were lined up in a neat little ring around Earth!"

Edgerly nodded. "That all?"

"No, sir. This morning my scout force reported that ten more ships have taken positions around the planet!"

"Ships of New Gallia?"

"Ruthenian ones, sir."

Edgerly moistened his lips and looked around the room, at the hodgepodge of Cabinet members, Congressional leaders, presidential aides, military men. He wouldn't have been at all surprised to learn that a couple of newsmen had sneaked into the conference too.

"Nine New Gallian ships, ten Ruthenian ones," he repeated. "Just hanging up there in orbit? Not doing anything?"

"That's right, sir."

"Okay. Scram, all of you! This is a serious matter, and

it has to be dealt with at once." He glanced at his watch. The time was 1300. Figure two hours for preparing his speech, he thought.

"You can announce that I'll address a special joint session of Congress at 1500 sharp," the President said.

Congress assembled. Congress listened. And when President Edgerly demanded special power to deal with the crisis, Congress gave it to him.

"It's not that I'm anxious to plunge this world into war," he said ringingly. "But Columbia's pride must be upheld! Two alien powers are menacing the planet from which our ancestors sprang, the planet on which the finest form of government known to man evolved."

Applause.

"Many of us have visited Earth," Edgerly continued. "Many of us have stood before the gleaming shaft of marble that symbolizes for us the nation of our ancestors, the nation whose democratic traditions we uphold today. I speak, of course of the Washington Monument."

Thunderous applause.

"This very moment, ships of alien worlds fly over Earth. Their reason for this occupation we have not yet determined; at present, their intent is unknown. But Columbia must not remain asleep! Our ships must be present there, too!"

Wild applause.

"It may be that the worlds of New Gallia and Novaya Ruthenia plan to coalesce against us; it may be that their aims are wholly peaceful. Perhaps our shrine on Earth will be destroyed—but it will not be destroyed with impunity!"

A standing ovation followed.

That evening, thirteen WZ-1 warp-drive warships left Columbia, armed to the teeth. The Columbians were determined to see at close range just what devious plans the foreigners were laying.

The Hrossai, who lived on the fourth world of Alpha Centauri, were a race of beetle-browed humanoids with dull, smoldering eyes and flaky grayish skin. As one of the few intelligent races of nonhumans in the galaxy, they were objects of a certain amount of mild curiosity, but no one paid much attention to their activities.

A team of Terran sociologists had studied them, and had prepared an interesting report on their characteristics and attitudes. The report was even more interesting when it was projected five or six years into the future—but, naturally, the Terrans never bothered to show the report to any authorities on Columbia, New Gallia, or Novaya Ruthenia. They wouldn't have taken it very seriously anyway; the Terrans were good flute players and wrote some passable poetry, but their "science" was considered beneath contempt throughout the galaxy.

So when the Hrossai began their drive for galactic empire, the Terrans were the only ones who anticipated the attack. And Terra—the only prepared world—was the first to be assaulted.

The Hrossai, figuring the gentle people of Earth for a soft touch, sent only ten ships, and thought they were being extravagant at that.

But Terra was guarded—and had been for four years —by thirty-two fully armed warships, each manned by a crew made trigger-happy by four years of political friction and nerve-grinding inaction.

"It was a short war," Jorun Kedrik remarked. He and his companion Amsler had taken a transatlantic jaunt just after the brief, spectacular duel in the skies, and now were staring upward at the towering bulk of the Washington Monument.

Amsler chuckled. "Shortest war on record, I'll bet. It couldn't have taken more than ten minutes for our protectors to destroy the Hrossai ships, eh?"

"Hmm. Yes," Kedrik said. He studied the contours of the needle of marble before him. "It's certainly prettier than the Eiffel, anyway."

"Huh?"

"Just uttering esthetic judgments, that's all." He grinned. "You'll have to admit the plan worked out perfectly, though. If we had appealed to any of the three colonies for help, they would have shrugged it off—or they might have sent a ship or two. But by shifting emphasis to their holy places, and by playing them off against each other, we managed to get a first-rate little space navy, free of charge! You know, Earth beat the Hrossai without ever firing a single shot?"

A tiny dot of black appeared against the bright blue far above them—and, as the sun's rays struck it, it glittered.

"What's that?" Amsler asked.

"Probably a Columbian ship, guarding the Monument from Ruthenian attack," Kedrik said. "The saps *still* haven't caught wise, and I guess they're going to protect us forever. Well, it's simpler than maintaining fleets of our own, I suppose."

"Hey, mind if I snap a few photos?" a loud, rasping voice shouted suddenly.

The two Earthmen turned toward the newcomer. He was a tourist, broad, bulky, and heavily tanned—obviously a Columbian come to visit the Monument. He was waving a complex-looking stereocam at them.

"Shall we?" Amsler asked doubtfully.

"Course! The tourist wants a few snapshots of us simple native folk. Why shouldn't we oblige him, so he'll have a record of our primitive pastoral ways?"

Kedrik started to laugh, and after a moment Amsler joined in.

The Columbian drew near, focusing his camera. "What's the joke?" he asked. "What's so funny?"

"Nothing," Kedrik gasped between chuckles. "Just— an old Terran joke. Very obscure. You wouldn't get it."

"I'll bet the joke's on me," the tourist said good-naturedly. "Well, I don't care. Would you mind standing over there, by the Monument? It'll make a nice shot to show back home."

Ringing the Changes

There has been a transmission error in the shunt room, and several dozen bodies have been left without minds, while several dozen minds are held in the stasis net, unassigned and, for the moment, unassignable. Things like this have happened before, which is why changers take out identity insurance, but never has it happened to so many individuals at the same time. The shunt is postponed. Everyone must be returned to his original identity; then they will start over. Suppressing the news has proved to be impossible. The area around the hospital has been besieged by the news media. Hovercameras stare rudely at the building at every altitude from twelve to twelve hundred feet. Trucks are angle-parked in the street. Journalists trade tips, haggle with hospital personnel for the names of the bereaved, and seek to learn the identities of those involved in the mishap. "If I knew, I'd tell you," says Jaime Rodriguez, twenty-seven. "Don't you think I could use the money? But we don't know. That's the whole trouble, we don't know. The data tank was the first thing to blow."

The shunt room has two antechambers, one on the west side of the building, the other facing Broadway; one is occupied by those who believe they are related to the victims, while in the other can be found the men from the insurance companies. Like everyone else, the insurance men have no real idea of the victims' names, but they do know that various clients of theirs were due for shunting today, and with so many changers snarled up at once, the identity-insurance claims may ultimately run into the millions. The insurance men confer agitatedly with one another, dictate muttered memoranda, scream telephone calls into their cufflinks, and show other signs of distress, although several of them remain cool enough to conduct ordinary business while here; they place stock market orders and negotiate assignations with nurses. It is, however, a tense and difficult situation, whose final implications are yet unknown.

Dr. Vardaman appears, perspired, paternal. "We're making every effort," he says, "to reunite each changer with the proper identity matrix. I'm fully confident. Only a matter of time. Your loved ones, safe and sound."

"We aren't the relatives," says one of the insurance men.

"Excuse me," says Dr. Vardaman, and leaves.

The insurance men wink and tap their temples knowingly. They peer beyond the antechamber door.

"Cost us a fortune," one broker says.

"Not your money," an adjuster points out.

"Raise premiums, I guess."

"Lousy thing. Lousy thing. Lousy thing. Could have been me."

"You a changer?"

"Due for a shunt next Tuesday."

"Tough luck, man. You could have used a vacation."

The antechamber door opens. A plump woman with dark-shadowed eyes enters. "Where are they?" she asks. "I want to see them! My husband was shunting today!"

She begins to sob and then to shriek. The insurance men rush to comfort her. It will be a long and somber day.

NOW GO ON WITH THE STORY

After a long time in the stasis net, the changer decides that something must have gone wrong with the shunt. It has never taken this long before. Something as simple as a shift of persona should be accomplished quickly, like the pulling of a tooth: *out, shunt, in.* Yet minutes or possibly hours have gone by, and the shunt has not come. What are they waiting for? I paid good money for a shunt. Something wrong somewhere, I bet.

Get me out of here. Change me.

The changer has no way of communicating with the hospital personnel. The changer, at present, exists only as a pattern of electrical impulses held in the stasis net. In theory it is possible for an expert to communicate in code even across the stasis gap, lighting up nodes on a talkboard; it was in this way that preliminary research into changing was carried out. But this changer has no such skills, being merely a member of the lay public seeking temporary identity transformation, a holiday sojourn in another's skull. The changer must wait in limbo.

A voice impinges. "This is Dr. Vardaman, addressing all changers in the net. There's been a little technical difficulty, here. What we need to do now is put you all back in the bodies you started from, which is just a routine reverse shunt, as you know, and when everybody is sorted out we can begin again. Clear? So the next thing that's going to happen to you is that you'll get shunted, only you won't be changed, heh-heh, at least we don't *want* you to be changed. As soon as you're able to speak to us, please tell your nurse if you're back in the right body, so we can disconnect you from the master switchboard, all right? Here we go, now, one, two, three—"

* * *

—shunt.

This body is clearly the wrong one, for it is female. The changer trembles, taking possession of the cerebral fibers and driving pitons into the autonomic nervous system. A hand rises and touches a breast. Erectile tissue responds. The skin is soft and the flesh is firm. The changer strokes a cheek. Beardless. He searches now for vestigial personality traces. He finds a name, Vonda Lou, and the image of a street, wide and dusty, a small town in a flat region, with squat square-fronted buildings set well back from the pavement, and gaudy automobiles parked sparsely in front of them. Beyond the town the zone of dry red earth begins; far away are the bare brown mountains. This is no place for the restless. A soothing voice says, "They catch us, Vonda Lou, they gonna take a baseball bat, jam it you know where," and Vonda Lou replies, "They ain't gone catch us anyway," and the other voice says, "But if they do, but if they do?" The room is warm but not humid. There are crickets outside. Cars without mufflers roar by. Vonda Lou says, "Stop worrying and put your head here. *Here.* That's it. Oh, nice—" There is a giggle. They change positions. Vonda Lou says, "No fellow ever did that to you, right?" The soft voice says, "Oh, Vonda Lou—" And Vonda Lou says, "One of these days we gone get out of this dime-store town—" Her hands clutch yielding flesh. In her mind dances the image of a drum majorette parading down the dusty main street, twirling a baton, lifting knees high and pulling the white shorts tight over the smug little rump, yes, yes, look at those things jiggle up there, look all the nice stuff, and the band plays *Dixie* and the football team comes marching by, and Vonda Lou laughs, thinking of that big hulking moron and how he had tried to dirty her, putting his paws all over her, that dumb Billy Joe who figured he was going to score, and all the time Vonda Lou was laughing at him inside, because it wasn't the halfback but the drum majorette who had what she wanted, and—

Voice: "Can you hear me? If there has been a proper

matching of body and mind, please raise your right hand."
The changer lifts left hand.

* * *

—*shunt*
The world here is dark green within a fifty-yard radius of the helmet lamp, black beyond. The temperature is 38 degrees F. The pressure is six atmospheres. One moves like a crab within one's jointed suit, scuttling along the bottom. Isolated clumps of gorgonians wave in the current. To the left, one can see as though through a funnel the cone of light that rises to the surface, where the water is blue. Along the face of the submerged cliff are coral outcroppings, but not here, not this deep, where sunlight never reaches and the sea is of a primal coldness.

One moves cautiously, bothered by the pressure drag. One clutches one's collecting rod tightly, stepping over nodules of manganese and silicon, swinging the lamp in several directions, searching for the place where the bottom drops away. One is uneasy and edgy here, not because of the pressure or the dark or the chill, but because one is cursed with an imagination, and one cannot help but think of the kraken in the pit. One dreams of Tennyson's dreamless beast, below the thunders of the upper deep. Faintest sunlights flee about his shadowy sides: above him swell huge sponges of millennial growth and height.

One comes now to the brink of the abyss.

There hath he lain for ages and will lie, battening upon huge seaworms in his sleep, until the latter fire shall heat the deep; then once by man and angels to be seen, in roaring he shall rise and on the surface die. Yes. One is moved, yes. One inclines one's lamp, hoping its beam will strike a cold glittering eye below. Far, far beneath in the abysmal sea. There is no sign of the thick ropy tentacles, the mighty beak.

"Going down in, now," one says to those above.

One has humor as well as imagination. One pauses at the brink, picks up a chalky stone, inscribes on a boulder crusted with the tracks of worms the single word:

NEMO

One laughs and flips aside the stone, and launches one's self into the abyss, kicking off hard against the continental shelf. Down. And down. Seeking wondrous grot and secret cell.

The changer sighs, thinking of debentures floated on the Zurich exchange, of contracts for future delivery of helium and plutonium, of puts and calls and margins. He will not enter the abyss; he will not see the kraken; feebly he signals with his left hand.

* * *

—shunt

A middle-aged male, at least. There's hope in that. A distinct paunch at the middle. Some shortness of breath. Faint stubble on face. The legs feel heavy, with swollen feet; a man gets tired easily at a certain age, when his responsibilities are heavy. The sound of unanswered telephones rings in his ears. Everything is familiar: the tensions, the frustrations, the fatigue, the sense of things unfinished and things uncommenced, the staleness in the mouth, the emptiness in the gut. This must be the one. Home again, all too soon?

Q: Sir, in the event of an escalation of the crisis, would you request an immediate meeting of the Security Council, or would you attempt to settle matters through quasi-diplomatic means as was done in the case of the dispute between Syria and the Maldive Islands?

A: Let's not put the horse in the cart, shall we?

Q: According to last Monday's statement by the Bureau of the Budget, this year's deficit is already running twelve billion ahead of last, and we're only halfway through the second quarter. Have you given any concern to the accusation of the Fiscal Responsibility Party that this is the result of a deliberate Communist-dictated plan to demoralize the economy?

A: What do you think?

Q: Is there any thought of raising the tax on personality-shunting?

A: Well, now, there's already a pretty steep tax on that, and we don't want to do anything that'll interfere with the rights of American citizens to move around from body to body, as is their God-given and constitutional right. So I don't think we'll change that tax any.

Q: Sir, we understand that you yourself have done some shunting. We—

A: Where'd you hear that?

Q: I think it was Representative Spear, of Iowa, who said the other day that it's well known that the President visits a shunt room every time he's in New York, and—

A: You know these Republicans. They'll say anything at all about a Democrat.

Q: Mr. President, does the Administration have any plans for ending sexual discrimination in public washrooms?

A: I've asked the Secretary of the Interior to look into that, inasmuch as it might involve interstate commerce and also being on Federal property, and we expect a report at a later date.

Q: Thank you, Mr. President.

The left hand stirs and rises. Not this one, obviously. The hand requests a new phase-shift. The body is properly soggy and decayed, yes. But one must not be deceived by superficialities. This is the wrong one. Out, please. Out.

* * *

—*shunt*

The crowd stirred in anticipation as Bernie Kingston left the on-deck circle and moved toward the plate, and by the time he was in the batter's box they were standing.

Kingston glanced out at the imposing figure of Ham Fillmore, the lanky Hawks southpaw on the mound. *Go ahead,* Bernie thought. *I'm ready for you.*

He wiggled the bat back and forth two or three times and dug in hard, waiting for the pitch. It was a low, hard fastball, delivered by way of first base, and it shot past him before he had a chance to offer. "Strike one," he heard. He looked down toward third to see if the manager had any sign for him.

But Danner was staring at him blankly. *You're on your own,* he seemed to be saying.

The next pitch was right in the groove, and Bernie lined it effortlessly past the big hurler's nose and on into right field for a single. The crowd roared its approval as he trotted down to first.

"Good going, kid," said Jake Edwards, the first-base coach, when Bernie got there. Bernie grinned. Base hits always felt good, and he loved to hear the crowd yell.

The Hawks' catcher came out to the mound and called a conference. Bernie wandered around first, doing some gardening with his spikes. With one out and the score tied in the eighth, he couldn't blame the Hawks for wanting to play it close to the belt.

As soon as the mound conference broke up it was the

Stags' turn to call time. "Come here, kid," Jake Edwards called.

"What's the big strategy this time?" Bernie asked boredly.

"No lip, kid. Just go down on the second pitch."

Bernie shrugged and edged a few feet off the base. Ham Fillmore was still staring down at his catcher, shaking off signs, and Karl Folsom, the Stag cleanup man, was waiting impatiently at the plate.

"Take a lead," the coach whispered harshly. "Go on, Kingston—get down that line."

The hurler finally was satisfied with his sign, and he swung into the windup. The pitch was a curve, breaking far outside. Folsom didn't venture at it, and the ball hit the dirt and squirted through the catcher's big mitt. It trickled about fifteen feet back of the plate.

Immediately the Hawks' shortstop moved in to cover second in case Bernie might be going. But Bernie had no such ideas. He stayed put at first.

"What's the matter, lead in ya pants?" called a derisive voice from the Hawk dugout.

Bernie snarled something and returned to the base. He glanced over at third, and saw Danner flash the steal sign.

He leaned away from first cautiously, five, six steps, keeping an eye cocked at the mound.

The pitcher swung into a half-windup—Bernie broke for second—his spikes dug furiously into the dusty basepath—

Out! Out! Out! The left hand upraised! Not this one, either! Out! Get me out!

* * *

—shunt
Through this mind go dreams of dollars, and the changer believes they have finally made the right match-up. He

takes the soundings and finds much here that is familiar. Dow-Jones Industrials 1453.28, down 8.29. Confirmation of the bear signal by the rails. Penetration of the August 13 lows. Watch the arbitrage spread you get by going short on the common while picking up 10,000 of the $1.50 convertible preferred at—

The substance is right; so is the context. But the tone is wrong, the changer realizes. This man loves his work.

The changer tours this man's mind from the visitors' gallery.

—we can unload 800 shares in Milan at 48, which gives us two and a half points right there, and then after they announce the change in redemption ratio I think we ought to drop another thousand on the Zurich board—

—give me those Tokyo quotes! Damn you, you sleepy bastard, don't slow me up! Here, here, Kansai Electric Power, I want the price in yen, not the American Depositary crap—

—pick up twenty-two percent of the voting shares through street names before we announce the tender offer, that's the right way to do it, then hit them hard from a position of strength and watch the board of directors fold up in two days—

—I think we can work it with the participating preference stock, if we give them just a little hint that the dividend might go up in January, and of course they don't have to know that after the merger we're going to throw them all out anyway, so—

—why am I in it? Why, for the fun of it!—

Yes. The sheer joy of wielding power. The changer lingers here, sadly wondering why it is that this man, who after all functions in the same environment as the changer himself, shows such fierce gusto, such delight in finance for the sake of finance, while the changer derives only sour tastes and dull aches from all his getting. It's because he's so young, the changer decides. The thrill hasn't yet worn off for him. The changer surveys the body in which he is temporarily a resident. He makes himself aware of the flat belly's firm musculature, of the even rhythms of the heart, of the lean flanks. This man is at most forty years old, the changer concludes. Give him thirty more years and ten million more dollars and he'll know how hollow it all is. The futility of existence, the changer thinks. You feel it at seventeen, you feel it at seventy, but often you fail to feel it in between. I feel it. I feel it. And so this body can't be mine. Lift the left hand. Out.

*   *   *

"We are having some difficulties," Dr. Vardaman confesses, "in achieving accurate pairings of bodies and minds." He tells this to the insurance men, for there is every reason to be frank with them. "At the time of the transmission error we were left with—ah—twenty-nine minds in the stasis net. So far we've returned eleven of them to their proper bodies. The others—"

"Where are the eleven?" asks an adjuster.

"They're recuperating in the isolation ward," Dr. Vardaman replies. "You understand, they've been through three or four shunts apiece today, and that's pretty strenuous. After they've rested, we'll offer them the option to undergo the contracted-for change as scheduled, or to take a full refund."

"Meanwhile we got eighteen possible identity-insurance claims," says another of the insurance men. "That's something like fifteen million bucks. We got to know what you're doing to get the others back in the right bodies."

"Our efforts are continuing. It's merely a matter of time until everyone is properly matched."

"And if some of them die while you're shunting them?"

"What can I say?" Dr. Vardaman says. "We're making every attempt."

To the relatives he says, "There's absolutely no cause for alarm. Another two hours and we'll have it all straightened out. Please be assured that none of the clients involved are suffering any hardship or inconvenience, and in fact this may be a highly interesting and entertaining experience for them."

"My husband," the plump woman says. "Where's my husband?"

* * *

—shunt

The changer is growing weary of this. They have had him in five bodies, now. How many more times will they shove him about? Ten? Twenty? Sixteen thousand? He knows that he can free himself from this wheel of transformations at any time. Merely raise the right hand, claim a body as one's own. They'd never know. Walk right out of the hospital, threatening to sue everybody in sight; they scare easily and won't interfere. Pick your body. Be anyone who appeals to you. Pick fast, though, because if you wait too long they'll hit the right combination and twitch you back into the body you started from. Tired, defeated, old, do you want that?

Here's your chance, changer. Steal another man's body. Another woman's if that's your kick. You could have walked out of here as that dyke from Texas. Or that diver. That ballplayer. That hard young market sharpie. Or the President. Or this new one, now—take your pick, changer.

What do you want to be? Essence precedes existence. They offer you your choice of bodies. Why go back to your own? Why pick up a stale identity, full of old griefs?

The changer considers the morality of such a deed.

The chances are good of getting away with it. Others in this mess are probably doing the same thing; it's musical chairs with souls, and if eight or nine take the wrong bodies, they'll never get it untangled. Of course, if I switch, someone else switches and gets stuck with my body. Aging. Decrepit. Who wants to be a used-up stock-broker? On the other hand, the changer realizes, there are consolations. The body he wishes to abandon is wealthy, and that wealth would go to the body's claimant. Maybe someone thought of that already, and grabbed my identity. Maybe that's why I'm being shunted so often into these others. The shunt-room people can't find the right one.

The changer asks himself what his desires are.

To be young again? To play Faust? No. Not really. He wants to rest. He wants peace. There is no peace for him in returning to his proper self. Too many ghosts await him there. The changer's needs are special.

The changer examines this latest body into which he has been shunted.

Quite young. Male. Undergraduate, mind stuffed full of Kant, Hegel, Fichte, Kierkegaard. Wealthy family. Curling red hair; sleek limbs; thoughts of willing girls, holidays in Hawaii, final exams, next fall's clothing styles. Adonis on a lark, getting himself changed as a respite from the academic pace? But no: the changer probes more deeply and finds a flaw, a fatal one. There is anguish beneath the young man's self-satisfaction, and rightly so, for this body is defective, it is gravely marred. The changer is surprised and saddened, and then feels joy and relief, for this body fills his very need and more. He sees for himself the hope of peace with honor, a speedier exit, a good deed. It is a far, far better thing. He will volunteer.

His right hand rises. His eyes open.

"This is the one," he announces. "I'm home again!" His conscience is clear.

* * *

Once the young man was restored to his body, the doctors asked him if he still wished to undergo the change

he had contracted for. He was entitled to this one final
adventure, which they all knew would have to be his
last changing, since the destruction of the young man's
white corpuscles was nearly complete. No, he said, he had
had enough excitement during the mixup in the shunt
room, and craved no further changes. His doctors agreed
he was wise, for his body might not be able to stand the
strain of another shunt; and they took him back to the
terminal ward. Death came two weeks later, peacefully,
very peacefully.

Hawksbill Station

One

Barrett was the uncrowned king of Hawksbill Station. He had been there the longest; he had suffered the most; he had the deepest inner resources of strength. Before his accident, he had been able to whip any man in the place. Now he was a cripple, but he still had that aura of power that gave him command. When there were problems at the Station, they were brought to Barrett. That was axiomatic. He was the king.

He ruled over quite a kingdom, too. In effect it was the whole world, pole to pole, meridian to meridian. For what it was worth. It wasn't worth very much.

Now it was raining again. Barrett shrugged himself to his feet in the quick, easy gesture that cost him an infinite amount of carefully concealed agony, and shuffled to the door of his hut. Rain made him impatient: the pounding of those great greasy drops against the corrugated tin roof was enough even to drive a Jim Barrett loony. He nudged the door open. Standing in the doorway, Barrett looked out over his kingdom.

Barren rock, nearly to the horizon. A shield of raw dolomite going on and on. Raindrops danced and bounced on that continental slab of rock. No trees. No grass. Behind Barrett's hut lay the sea, gray and vast. The sky was gray too, even when it wasn't raining.

He hobbled out into the rain. Manipulating his crutch was getting to be a simple matter for him now. He leaned comfortably, letting his crushed left foot dangle. A rockslide had pinned him last year during a trip to the edge of the Inland Sea. Back home, Barrett would have been fitted with prosthetics and that would have been the end of it: a new ankle, a new instep, refurbished ligaments and tendons. But home was a billion years away, and home there's no returning.

The rain hit him hard. Barrett was a big man, six and a half feet tall, with hooded dark eyes, a jutting nose, a chin that was a monarch among chins. He had weighed two hundred fifty pounds in his prime, in the good old agitating days when he had carried banners and pounded out manifestos. But now he was past sixty and beginning to shrink a little, the skin getting loose around the places where the mighty muscles used to be. It was hard to keep your weight in Hawksbill Station. The food was nutritious, but it lacked intensity. A man got to miss steak. Eating brachiopod stew and trilobite hash wasn't the same thing at all. Barrett was past all bitterness, though. That was another reason why the men regarded him as the leader. He didn't scowl. He didn't rant. He was resigned to his fate, tolerant of eternal exile, and so he could help the others get over that difficult, heart-clawing period of transition.

A figure arrived, jogging through the rain: Norton. The doctrinaire Khrushchevist with the Trotskyite leanings. A small, excitable man who frequently appointed himself messenger whenever there was news at the Station. He sprinted toward Barrett's hut, slipping and sliding over the naked rocks.

Barrett held up a meaty hand. "Whoa, Charley. Take it easy or you'll break your neck!"

Norton halted in front of the hut. The rain had pasted the widely spaced strands of his brown hair to his skull.

His eyes had the fixed, glossy look of fanaticism—or perhaps just astigmatism. He gasped for breath and staggered into the hut, shaking himself like a wet puppy. He obviously had run all the way from the main building of the Station, three hundred yards away—a long dash over rock that slippery.

"Why are you standing around in the rain?" Norton asked.

"To get wet," said Barrett, following him inside. "What's the news?"

"The Hammer's glowing. We're getting company."

"How do you know it's a live shipment?"

"It's been glowing for half an hour. That means they're taking precautions. They're sending a new prisoner. Anyway, no supplies shipment is due."

Barrett nodded. "Okay. I'll come over. If it's a new man, we'll bunk him in with Latimer."

Norton managed a rasping laugh. "Maybe he's a materialist. Latimer will drive him crazy with all that mystic nonsense. We could put him with Altman instead."

"And he'll be raped in half an hour."

"Altman's off that kick now," said Norton. "He's trying to create a real woman, not looking for second-rate substitutes."

"Maybe our new man doesn't have any spare ribs."

"Very funny, Jim." Norton did not look amused. "You know what I want the new man to be? A conservative, that's what. A black-souled reactionary straight out of Adam Smith. God, that's what I want!"

"Wouldn't you be happy with a fellow Bolshevik?"

"This place is full of Bolsheviks," said Norton. "Of all shades from pale pink to flagrant scarlet. Don't you think I'm sick of them? Sitting around fishing for trilobites and discussing the relative merits of Kerensky and Malenkov? I need someboy to *talk* to, Jim. Someboy I can fight with."

"All right," Barrett said, slipping into his rain gear. "I'll see what I can do about hocusing a debating partner out of the Hammer for you. A rip-roaring Objectivist, okay?"

He laughed. "You know something, maybe there's been a revolution Up Front since we got our last man? Maybe the left is in and the right is out, and they'll start shipping us nothing *but* reactionaries. How would you like that? Fifty or a hundred storm troopers, Charley? Plenty of material to debate economics with. And the place will fill up with more and more of them, until we're outnumbered, and then maybe they'll have a *putsch* and get rid of all the stinking leftists sent here by the old regime, and—"

Barrett stopped. Norton was staring at him in amazement, his faded eyes wide, his hand compulsively smoothing his thinning hair to hide his embarrassment. Barrett realized that he had just committed one of the most heinous crimes possible at Hawksbill Station: he had started to run off at the mouth. There hadn't been any call for his little outburst. What made it more troublesome was the fact that *he* was the one who had permitted himself such a luxury. He was supposed to be the strong one of this place, the stabilizer, the man of absolute integrity and principle and sanity on whom the others could lean. And suddenly he had lost control. It was a bad sign. His dead foot was throbbing again; possibly that was the reason.

In a tight voice he said, "Let's go. Maybe the new man is here already."

They stepped outside. The rain was beginning to let up; the storm was moving out to sea. In the east, over what would one day be the Atlantic, the sky was still clotted with gray mist, but to the west a different grayness was emerging, the shade of normal gray that meant dry weather. Before he had come out here, Barrett had expected to find the sky practically black, because there'd be fewer dust particles to bounce the light around and turn things blue. But the sky seemed to be a weary beige. So much for a priori theories.

Through the thinning rain they walked toward the main building. Norton accommodated himself to Barrett's limping pace, and Barrett, wielding his crutch furiously, did his damndest not to let his infirmity slow them up. He nearly lost his footing twice, and fought hard not to let Norton see.

Hawksbill Station spread out before them.

It covered about five hundred acres. In the center of everything was the main building, an ample dome that contained most of their equipment and supplies. At widely spaced intervals, rising from the rock shield like grotesque giant green mushrooms, were the plastic blisters of the individual dwellings. Some, like Barrett's, were shielded by tin sheeting salvaged from shipments from Up Front. Others stood unprotected, just as they had come from the mouth of the extruder.

The huts numbered about eighty. At the moment, there were 140 inmates in Hawksbill Station, pretty close to the all-time high. Up Front hadn't sent back any hut-building materials for a long time, and so all the newer arrivals had to double up with bunkmates. Barrett and all those whose exile had begun before 2014 had the privilege of private dwellings, if they wanted them. (Some did not wish to live alone; Barrett, to preserve his own authority, felt that he was required to.) As new exiles arrived, they bunked in with those who currently lived alone, in reverse order of seniority. Most of the 2015 exiles had been forced to take roommates now. Another dozen deportees and the 2014 group would be doubling up. Of course, there were deaths all up and down the line, and there were plenty who were eager to have company in their huts.

Barrett felt, though, that a man who has been sentenced to life imprisonment ought to have the privilege of privacy, if he desires it. One of his biggest problems here was keeping people from cracking up because there was too little privacy. Propinquity could be intolerable in a place like this.

Norton pointed toward the big shiny-skinned green dome of the main building. "There's Altman going in now. And Rudiger. And Hutchett. Something's happening!"

Barrett stepped up his pace. Some of the men entering the building saw his bulky figure coming over the rise in the rock, and waved to him. Barrett lifted a massive hand in reply. He felt mounting excitement. It was a big event at the Station whenever a new man arrived. Nobody had come for six months, now. That was the longest gap he could remember. It had started to seem as though no one would ever come again.

That would be a catastrophe. New men were all that stood between the older inmates and insanity. New men brought news from the future, news from the world that was eternally left behind. They contributed new personalities to a group that always was in danger of going stale.

And, Barrett knew, some men—he was not one—lived in the deluded hope that the next arrival might just be a woman.

That was why they flocked to the main building when the Hammer began to glow. Barrett hobbled down the path. The rain died away just as he reached the entrance.

Within, sixty or seventy Station residents crowded the chamber of the Hammer—just about every man in the place who was able in body and mind, and still alert enough to show curiosity about a newcomer. They shouted their greetings to Barrett. He nodded, smiled, deflected their questions with amiable gestures.

"Who's it going to be this time, Jim?"

"Maybe a girl, huh? Around nineteen years old, blonde, built like—"

"I hope he can play stochastic chess, anyway."

"Look at the glow! It's deepening!"

Barrett, like the others, stared at the Hammer. The complex, involuted collection of unfathomable instruments burned a bright cherry-red now, betokening the surge of who knew how many kilowatts being pumped in at the far end of the line. The glow had spread to the Anvil now, that broad aluminum bedplate on which all shipments from the future were dropped. In another moment—

"Condition Crimson!" somebody yelled. "Here he comes!"

Two

Two billion years up the time-line, power was flooding into the real Hammer of which this was only the partial replica. A man—or something else—stood in the center of the real Anvil, waiting for the Hawksbill Field to enfold him and kick him back to the early Paleozoic. The effect of time travel was very much like being hit with a gigantic hammer and driven clear through the walls of the continuum: hence the governing metaphors for the parts of the machine.

Setting up Hawksbill Station had been a long, slow job. The Hammer had knocked a pathway and had sent back the nucleus of the receiving station, first. Since there was no receiving station on hand to receive the receiving station, a certain amount of waste had occurred. It wasn't necessary to have a Hammer and Anvil on the receiving end, except as a fine control to prevent temporal spread; without the equipment, the field wandered a little, and it was possible to scatter consecutive shipments over a span of twenty or thirty years. There was plenty of such temporal garbage all around Hawksbill Station: stuff that had been intended for the original installation, but which because of tuning imprecisions in the pre-Hammer days had landed a couple of decades (and a couple of hundred miles) away from the intended site.

Despite such difficulties, they had finally sent through enough components to the master temporal site to allow for the construction of a receiving station. Then the first prisoners had gone through: technicians who knew how to put the Hammer and Anvil together. Of course, it was their privilege to refuse to cooperate. But it was in their own advantage to assemble the receiving station, thus making it possible for them to be sure of getting further supplies from Up Front. They had done the job. After that, outfitting Hawksbill Station had been easy.

Now the Hammer glowed, meaning that they had activated the Hawksbill Field on the sending end, somewhere up around 2028 or 2030 A.D. All the sending was done there. All the receiving was done here. It didn't work the other way. Nobody really knew why, although there was a lot of superficially profound talk about the rules of entropy.

There was a whining, hissing sound as the edges of the Hawksbill Field began to ionize the atmosphere in the room. Then came the expected thunderclap of implosion, caused by an imperfect overlapping of the quantity of air that was subtracted from this era and the quantity that was being thrust into it. And then, abruptly, a man dropped out of the Hammer and lay, stunned and limp, on the gleaming Anvil.

He looked young, which surprised Barrett considerably. He seemed to be well under thirty. Generally, only middle-aged men were sent to Hawksbill Station. Incorrigibles, who had to be separated from humanity for the general good. The youngest man in the place now had been close to forty when he arrived. The sight of this lean, clean-cut boy drew a hiss of anguish from a couple of the men in the room, and Barrett understood the constellation of emotions that pained them.

The new man sat up. He stirred like a child coming out of a long, deep sleep. He looked around.

His face was very pale. His thin lips seemed bloodless. His blue eyes blinked rapidly. His jaws worked as though he wanted to say something, but could not find the words.

There were no physiological harmful effects to time travel, but it could be a rough jolt to the consciousness. The last moments before the Hammer descended were very much like the final moments beneath the guillotine, since exile to Hawksbill Station was tantamount to a sentence of death. The departing prisoner took his last look at the world of rocket transport and artificial organs, at the world in which he had lived and loved and agitated for a political cause, and then he was rammed into the inconceivably remote past on a one-way journey. It was a gloomy business, and it was not very surprising that the newcomers arrived in a state of emotional shock.

Barrett elbowed his way through the crowd. Automatically, the others made way for him. He reached the lip of the Anvil and leaned over it, extending a hand to the new man. His broad smile was met by a look of blank bewilderment.

"I'm Jim Barrett. Welcome to Hawksbill Station. Here —get off that thing before a load of groceries lands on top of you." Wincing a little as he shifted his weight, Barrett pulled the new man down from the Anvil. It was altogether likely for the idiots Up Front to shoot another shipment along a minute after sending a man.

Barrett beckoned to Mel Rudiger, and the plump anarchist handed the new man an alcohol capsule. He took it and pressed it to his arm without a word. Charley Norton offered him a candy bar. The man shook it off. He looked groggy—a real case of temporal shock, Barrett thought, possibly the worst he had ever seen. The newcomer hadn't even spoken yet. Could the effect really be that extreme?

Barrett said, "We'll go to the infirmary and check you out. Then I'll assign you your quarters. There's time for you to find your way around and meet everybody later on. What's your name?"

"Hahn. Lew Hahn."

"I can't hear you."

"Hahn," the man repeated, still only barely audible.

"When are you from, Lew?"

"2029."

"You feel pretty sick?"

"I feel awful. I don't even believe this is happening to me. There's no such place as Hawksbill Station, is there?

"I'm afraid there is," Barrett said. "At least, for most of us. A few of the boys think it's all an illusion induced by drugs. But I have my doubts of that. If it's an illusion, it's damned good. Look."

He put one arm around Hahn's shoulders and guided him through the press of prisoners, out of the Hammer chamber and toward the nearby infirmary. Although Hahn looked thin, even fragile, Barrett was surprised to feel the rippling muscles in those shoulders. He suspected that this man was a lot less helpless and ineffectual than he seemed to be right now. He *had* to be, if he had earned banishment to Hawksbill Station.

They passed the open door of the building. "Look out there," Barrett commanded.

Hahn looked. He passed a hand across his eyes as though to clear away unseen cobwebs, and looked again.

"A Late Cambrian landscape," said Barrett quietly. "This view would be a geologist's dream, except that geologists don't tend to become political prisoners, it seems. Out in front of you is what they call Appalachia. It's a strip of rock a few hundred miles wide and a few thousand miles long, running from the Gulf of Mexico to Newfoundland. To the east we've got the Atlantic Ocean. A little way to the west we've got a thing called the Appalachian Geosyncline, which is a trough five hundred miles wide full of water. Somewhere about two thousand miles to the west there's another trough, what they call the Cordilleran Geosyncline. It's full of water too, and at this particular stage of geological history the patch of land between the geosynclines is below sea level, so where Appalachia ends we've got the Inland Sea, currently, running way out to the west. On the far side of the Inland Sea is a narrow north-south land mass called Cascadia, that's going to be California and Oregon and Washington someday. Don't hold your breath till it happens. I hope you like seafood, Lew."

Hahn stared, and Barrett, standing beside him at the doorway, stared also. You never got used to the alienness of this place, not even after you had lived here twenty years, as Barrett had. It was Earth, and yet it was not really Earth at all, because it was somber and empty and unreal. The gray oceans swarmed with life, of course. But there was nothing on land except occasional patches of moss in the occasional patches of soil that had formed on the bare rock. Even a few cockroaches would be welcome; but insects, it seemed, were still a couple of geological periods in the future. To land dwellers, this was a dead world, a world unborn.

Shaking his head, Hahn moved away from the door. Barrett led him down the corridor and into the small, brightly lit room that served as the infirmary. Doc Quesada was waiting. Quesada wasn't really a doctor, but he had been a medical technician once, and that was good enough. He was a compact, swarthy man with a look of complete self-assurance. He hadn't lost too many patients, all things considered. Barrett had watched him removing appendices with total aplomb. In his white smock, Quesada looked sufficiently medical to fit the role.

Barrett said, "Doc, this is Lew Hahn. He's in temporal shock. Fix him up."

Quesada nudged the newcomer onto a webfoam cradle and unzipped his blue jersey. Then he reached for his medical kit. Hawksbill Station was well equipped for most medical emergencies, now. The people Up Front had no wish to be inhumane, and they sent back all sorts of useful things, like anesthetics and surgical clamps and medicines and dermal probes. Barrett could remember a time at the beginning when there had been nothing much here but the empty huts, and a man who hurt himself was in real trouble.

"He's had a drink already," said Barrett.

"I see that," Quesada murmured. He scratched at his short-cropped, bristly mustache. The little diagnostat in the cradle had gone rapidly to work, flashing information about Hahn's blood pressure, potassium count, dilation index, and much else. Quesada seemed to comprehend the barrage of facts. After a moment he said to Hahn, "You aren't really sick, are you? Just shaken up a little. I don't blame you. Here—I'll give you a quick jolt to calm your nerves, and you'll be all right. As all right as any of us ever are."

He put a tube to Hahn's carotid and thumbed the snout. The subsonic whirred, and a tranquilizing compound slid into the man's bloodstream. Hahn shivered.

Quesada said, "Let him rest for five minutes. Then he'll be over the hump."

They left Hahn in his cradle and went out of the infirmary. In the hall, Barrett looked down at the little medic and said, "What's the report on Valdosto?"

Valdosto had gone into psychotic collapse several weeks before. Quesada was keeping him drugged and trying to bring him slowly back to the reality of Hawksbill Station. Shrugging, he replied, "The status is quo. I let him out from under the dream-juice this morning and he was the same as he's been."

"You don't think he'll come out of it?"

"I doubt it. He's cracked for keeps. They could paste him together Up Front, but—"

"Yeah," Barrett said. If he could get Up Front at all, Valdosto wouldn't have cracked. "Keep him happy, then. If he can't be sane, he can at least be comfortable. What about Altman? Still got the shakes?"

"He's building a woman," Quesada said.

"That's what Charley Norton told me. What's he using? A rag, a bone—"

"I gave him some surplus chemicals. Chosen for their color, mainly. He's got some foul green copper compounds and a little bit of ethyl alcohol and six or seven other things, and he collected some soil and threw in a lot of dead shellfish, and he's sculpting it all into what he claims is female shape and waiting for lightning to strike it."

"In other words, he's gone crazy," Barrett said.

"I think that's a safe assumption. But he's not molesting his friends any more, anyway. You didn't think his homosexual phase would last much longer, as I recall."

"No, but I didn't think he'd go off the deep end. If a man needs sex and he can find some consenting playmates here, that's quite all right with me. But when he starts putting a woman together out of some dirt and rotten brachiopod meat it means we've lost him. It's too bad."

Quesada's dark eyes flickered. "We're all going to go that way sooner or later, Jim."

"I haven't. You haven't."

"Give us time. I've only been here eleven years."

"Altman's been here only eight. Valdosto even less."

"Some shells crack faster than others," said Quesada. "Here's our new friend."

Hahn had come out of the infirmary to join them. He still looked pale, but the fright was gone from his eyes. He was beginning to adjust to the unthinkable.

He said, "I couldn't help overhearing your conversation. Is there a lot of mental illness here?"

"Some of the men haven't been able to find anything meaningful to do here," Barrett said. "It eats them away. Quesada here has his medical work. I've got administrative duties. A couple of the fellows are studying the sea life. We've got a newspaper to keep some busy. But there are always those who just let themselves slide into despair, and they crack up. I'd say we have thirty or forty certifiable maniacs here at the moment, out of 140 residents."

"That's not so bad," Hahn said. "Considering the inherent instability of the men who get sent here, and the unusual conditions of life here."

Barrett laughed. "Hey, you're suddenly pretty articulate, aren't you? What was in the stuff Doc Quesada jolted you with?"

"I didn't mean to sound superior," Hahn said quickly. "Maybe that came out a little too smug. I mean—"

"Forget it. What did you do Up Front, anyway?"

"I was an economist."

"Just what we need," said Quesada. "He can help us solve our balance-of-payments problem."

Barrett said, "If you were an economist, you'll have plenty to discuss here. This place is full of economic theorists who'll want to bounce their ideas off you. Some of them are almost sane, too. Come with me and I'll show you where you're going to stay."

Three

The path from the main building to the hut of Donald Latimer was mainly downhill, for which Barrett was grateful even though he knew that he'd have to negotiate the uphill return in a little while. Latimer's hut was on the eastern side of the Station, looking out over the ocean. They walked slowly toward it. Hahn was solicitous of Barrett's game leg, and Barrett was irritated by the exaggerated care the younger man took to keep pace with him.

He was puzzled by this Hahn. The man was full of seeming contradictions—showing up here with the worst case of arrival shock Barrett had ever seen, then snapping out of it with remarkable quickness; looking frail and shy, but hiding solid muscles inside his jersey; giving an outer appearance of incompetence, but speaking with calm control. Barrett wondered what this young man had done to earn him the trip to Hawksbill Station, but there was time for such inquiries later. All the time in the world.

Hahn said, "Is everything like this? Just rock and ocean?"

"That's all. Land life hasn't evolved yet. Everything's wonderfully simple, isn't it? No clutter. No urban sprawl. There's some moss moving onto land, but not much."

"And in the sea? Swimming dinosaurs?"

Barrett shook his head. "There won't be any vertebrates for millions of years. We don't even have fish yet, let alone reptiles out there. All we can offer is that which creepeth. Some shellfish, some big fellows that look like squids, and trilobites. Seven hundred billion different species of trilobites. We've got a man named Rudiger—he's the one who gave you the drink—who's making a collection of them. He's writing the world's definitive text on trilobites."

"But nobody will ever read it in—in the future."

"Up Front, we say."

"Up Front."

"That's the pity of it," said Barrett. "We told Rudiger to inscribe his book on imperishable plates of gold and hope that it's found by paleontologists. But he says the odds are against it. A billion years of geology will chew his plates to hell before they can be found."

Hahn sniffed. "Why does the air smell so strange?"

"It's a different mix," Barrett said. "We've analyzed it. More nitrogen, a little less oxygen, hardly any CO_2 at all. But that isn't really why it smells odd to you. The thing is, it's pure air, unpolluted by the exhalations of life. Nobody's been respiring into it but us lads, and there aren't enough of us to matter."

Smiling, Hahn said, "I feel a little cheated that it's so empty. I expected lush jungles of weird plants, and pterodactyls swooping through the air, and maybe a tyrannosaur crashing into a fence around the Station."

"No jungles. No pterodactyls. No tyrannosaurs. No fences. You didn't do your homework."

"Sorry."

"This is the Late Cambrian. Sea life exclusively."

"It was very kind of them to pick such a peaceful era as the dumping ground for political prisoners," Hahn said. "I was afraid it would be all teeth and claws."

"Kind, hell! They were looking for an era where we couldn't do any harm. That meant tossing us back before the evolution of mammals, just in case we'd accidentally get hold of the ancestor of all humanity and snuff him out. And while they were at it, they decided to stash us so far in the past that we'd be beyond all land life, on the theory that maybe even if we slaughtered a baby dinosaur it might affect the entire course of the future."

"They don't mind if we catch a few trilobites?"

"Evidently they think it's safe," Barrett said. "It looks as though they were right. Hawksbill Station has been here for twenty-five years, and it doesn't seem as though we've tampered with future history in any measurable way. Of course, they're careful not to send us any women."

"Why is that?"

"So we don't start reproducing and perpetuating ourselves. Wouldn't that mess up the time-lines? A successful human outpost in One Billion B.C., that's had all that time to evolve and mutate and grow? By the time the twenty-first century came around, our descendants would be in charge and the other kind of human being would probably be in penal servitude, and there'd be more paradoxes created than you could shake a trilobite at. So they don't send the women here. There's a prison camp for women, too, but it's a few hundred million years up the time line in the Late Silurian, and never the twain shall meet. That's why Ned Altman's trying to build a woman out of dust and garbage."

"God made Adam out of less."

"Altman isn't God," Barrett said. "That's the root of his whole problem. Look, here's the hut where you're going to stay. I'm rooming you with Don Latimer. He's a very sensitive, interesting, pleasant person. He used to be a physicist before he got into politics, and he's been here about a dozen years, and I might as well warn you that he's developed a strong and somewhat cock-eyed mystic streak lately. The fellow he was rooming with killed himself last year, and since then he's been trying to find some way out of here through extrasensory powers."

"Is he serious?"

"I'm afraid he is. And we try to take him seriously. We all humor each other at Hawksbill Station; it's the only way we avoid a mass psychosis. Latimer will probably try to get you to collaborate with him on his project. If you don't like living with him, I can arrange a transfer for you. But I want to see how he reacts to someone new at the Station. I'd like you to give him a chance."

"Maybe I'll even help him find his psionic gateway."

"If you do, take me along," said Barrett. They both laughed. Then he rapped at Latimer's door. There was no answer, and after a moment Barrett pushed the door open. Hawksbill Station had no locks.

Latimer sat in the middle of the bare rock floor, cross-legged, meditating. He was a slender, gentle-faced man just beginning to look old. Right now he seemed a million miles away, ignoring them completely. Hahn shrugged. Barrett put a finger to his lips. They waited in silence for a few minutes, and then Latimer showed signs of coming up from his trance.

He got to his feet in a single flowing motion, without using his hands. In a low, courteous voice he said to Hahn, "Have you just arrived?"

"Within the last hour. I'm Lew Hahn."

"Donald Latimer. I regret that I have to make your acquaintance in these surroundings. But maybe we won't have to tolerate this illegal imprisonment much longer."

Barrett said, "Don, Lew is going to bunk with you. I think you'll get along well. He was an economist in 2029 until they gave him the Hammer."

"Where did you live?" Latimer asked, animation coming into his eyes.

"San Francisco."

The glow faded. Latimer said, "Were you ever in Toronto? I'm from there. I had a daughter—she'd be twenty-three now, Nella Latimer—I wondered if you knew her."

"No. I'm sorry."

"It wasn't very likely. But I'd love to know what kind of a woman she became. She was a little girl when I last saw her. Now I guess she's married. Or perhaps they've sent her to the other Station. Nella Latimer—you're sure you didn't know her?"

Barrett left them together. It looked as though they'd get along. He told Latimer to bring Hahn up to the main building at dinner for introductions, and went out. A chilly drizzle had begun again. Barrett made his way slowly, painfully up the hill. It had been sad to see the light flicker from Latimer's eyes when Hahn said he didn't know his daughter. Most of the time, men at Hawksbill Station tried not to speak about their families, preferring to keep those tormenting memories well repressed. But the arrival of newcomers generally stirred old ties. There was never any news of relatives, and no way to obtain any, because it was impossible for the Station to communicate with anyone Up Front. No way to ask for the photo of a loved one, no way to request specific medicines, no way to obtain a certain book or a coveted tape. In a mindless, impersonal way, Up Front sent periodic shipments to the Station of things thought useful—reading matter, medical supplies, technical equipment, food. Occasionally they were startling in their generosity, as when they sent a case of Burgundy, or a box of sensory spools, or a recharger for the power pack. Such gifts usually meant a brief thaw in the world situation, which customarily produced a shortlived desire to be kind to the boys in Hawksbill Station. But they had a policy about sending information about relatives. Or about contemporary newspapers. Fine wine, yes; a tridim of a daughter who would never be seen again, no.

For all Up Front knew, there was no one alive in Hawksbill Station. A plague could have killed everyone off ten years ago, but there was no way of telling. That was why the shipments still came back. The government whirred and clicked with predictable continuity. The government, whatever else it might be, was not malicious. There were other kinds of totalitarianism beside bloody repressive tyranny.

Pausing at the top of the hill, Barrett caught his breath. Naturally, the alien air no longer smelled strange to him. He filled his lungs with it. Once again the rain ceased. Through the grayness came the sunshine, making the naked rocks sparkle. Barrett closed his eyes a moment and leaned on his crutch, and saw as though on an inner screen the creatures with many legs climbing up out of the sea, and the mossy carpets spreading, and the flowerless plants uncoiling and spreading their scaly branches, and the dull hides of eerie amphibians glistening on the shores, and the tropic heat of the coal-forming epoch descending like a glove over the world.

All that lay far in the future. Dinosaurs. Little chittering mammals. Pithecanthropus in the forests of Java. Sargon and Hannibal and Attila, and Orville Wright, and Thomas Edison, and Edmond Hawksbill. And finally a benign government that would find the thoughts of some men so intolerable that the only safe place to which they could be banished was a rock at the beginning of time. The government was too civilized to put men to death for subversive activities, and too cowardly to let them remain alive. The compromise was the living death of Hawksbill Station. A billion years of impassable time was suitable insulation even for the most nihilistic idea.

Grimacing a little, Barrett struggled the rest of the way back toward his hut. He had long since come to accept his exile, but accepting his ruined foot was another matter entirely. The idle wish to find a way to regain the freedom of his own time no longer possessed him; but he wished with all his soul that the blank-faced administrators Up Front would send back a kit that would allow him to rebuild his foot.

He entered his hut and flung his crutch aside, sinking

down instantly on his cot. There had been no cots when he had come to Hawksbill Station. He had come here in the fourth year of the Station, when there were only a dozen buildings and little in the way of creature comforts. It had been a miserable place, then, but the steady accretion of shipments from Up Front had made it relatively tolerable. Of the fifty or so prisoners who had preceded Barrett to Hawksbill, none remained alive. He had held highest seniority for almost ten years. Time moved here at a one-to-one correlation with time Up Front; the Hammer was locked on this point of time, so that Hahn, arriving here today more than twenty years after Barrett, had departed from a year Up Front more than twenty years after the time of Barrett's expulsion. Barrett had not had the heart to begin pumping Hahn for news of 2029 so soon. He would learn all he needed to know, and small cheer it would be, anyway.

Barrett reached for a book. But the fatigue of hobbling around the Station had taken more out of him than he realized. He looked at the page for a moment. Then he put it away, and closed his eyes and dozed.

Four

That evening, as every evening, the men of Hawksbill Station gathered in the main building for dinner and recreation. It was not mandatory, and some men chose to eat alone. But tonight nearly everyone who was in full possession of his faculties was there, because this was one of the infrequent occasions when a newcomer had arrived to be questioned about the world of men.

Hahn looked uneasy about his sudden notoriety. He seemed to be basically shy, unwilling to accept all the attention now being thrust upon him. There he sat in the middle of the group, while men twenty and thirty years his senior crowded in on him with their questions, and it was obvious that he wasn't enjoying the session.

Sitting to one side, Barrett took little part in the discussion. His curiosity about Up Front's ideological shifts had ebbed a long time ago. It was hard for him to realize that he had once been so passionately concerned about concepts like syndicalism and the dictatorship of the proletariat and the guaranteed annual wage that he had been willing to risk imprisonment over them. His concern for humanity had not waned, merely the degree of his involvement in the twenty-first century's political problems. After twenty years at Hawksbill Station, Up Front had become unreal to Jim Barrett, and his energies centered around the crises and challenges of what he had come to think of as "his own" time—the Late Cambrian.

So he listened, but more with an ear for what the talk revealed about Lew Hahn than for what it revealed about current events Up Front. And what it revealed about Lew Hahn was mainly a matter of what was not revealed.

Hahn didn't say much. He seemed to be feinting and evading.

Charley Norton wanted to know, "Is there any sign of a weakening of the phony conservatism yet? I mean, they've been promising the end of big government for thirty years, and it gets bigger all the time."

Hahn moved restlessly in his chair. "They still promise. As soon as conditions become stabilized—"

"Which is when?"

"I don't know. I suppose they're just making words."

"What about the Martian Commune?" demanded Sid Hutchett. "Have they been infiltrating agents onto Earth?"

"I couldn't really say."

"How about the Gross Global Product?" Mel Rudiger wanted to know. "What's its curve? Still holding level, or has it started to drop?"

Hahn tugged at his ear. "I think it's slowly edging down."

"Where does the index stand?" Rudiger asked. "The

last figures we had, for '25, it was at 909. But in four years—"

"It might be something like 875 now," said Hahn.

It struck Barrett as a little odd that an economist would be so hazy about the basic economic statistic. Of course, he didn't know how long Hahn had been imprisoned before getting the Hammer. Maybe he simply wasn't up on the recent figures. Barrett held his peace.

Charley Norton wanted to find out some things about the legal rights of citizens. Hahn couldn't tell him. Rudiger asked about the impact of weather control—whether the supposedly conservative government of liberators was still ramming programmed weather down the mouths of the citizens—and Hahn wasn't sure. Hahn couldn't rightly say much about the functions of the judiciary, whether it had recovered any of the power stripped from it by the Enabling Act of '18. He didn't have any comments to offer on the tricky subject of population control. In fact, his performance was striking for its lack of hard information.

"He isn't saying much at all," Charley Norton grumbled to the silent Barrett. "He's putting up a smokescreen. But either he's not telling what he knows, or he doesn't know."

"Maybe he's not very bright," Barrett suggested.

"What did he do to get here? He must have had some kind of deep commitment. But it doesn't show, Jim! He's an intelligent kid, but he doesn't seem plugged in to anything that ever mattered to any of us."

Doc Quesada offered a thought. "Suppose he isn't a political at all. Suppose they're sending a different kind of prisoner back here now. Axe murderers, or something. A quiet kid who very quietly chopped up sixteen people one Sunday morning. Naturally he isn't interested in politics."

Barrett shook his head. "I doubt that. I think he's just clamming up because he's shy or ill at ease. It's his first night here, remember. He's just been kicked out of his own world and there's no going back. He may have left a wife and baby behind, you know. He may simply not give a damn tonight about sitting up there and spouting the latest word on abstract philosophical theory, when all he wants to do is go off and cry his eyes out. I say we ought to leave him alone."

Quesada and Norton looked convinced. They shook their heads in agreement; but Barrett didn't voice his opinion to the room in general. He let the quizzing of Hahn continue until it petered out of its own accord. The men began to drift away. A couple of them went in back to convert Hahn's vague generalities into the lead story for the next handwritten edition of the Hawksbill Station *Times*. Rudiger stood on a table and shouted out that he was going night-fishing, and four men asked to join him. Charley Norton sought out his usual debating partner, the nihilist Ken Belardi, and reopened, like a festering wound, their discussion of planning versus chaos, which bored them both to the point of screaming. The nightly games of stochastic chess began. The loners who had made rare visits to the main building simply to see the new man went back to their huts to do whatever it was they did in them alone each night.

Hahn stood apart, fidgeting and uncertain.

Barrett went up to him. "I guess you didn't really want to be quizzed tonight," he said.

"I'm sorry I couldn't have been more informative. I've been out of circulation a while, you see."

"But you were politically active, weren't you?"

"Oh, yes," Hahn said. "Of course." He flicked his tongue over his lips. "What's supposed to happen now?"

"Nothing in particular. We don't have organized activities here. Doc and I are going out on sick call. Care to join us?"

"What does it involve?" Hahn asked.

"Visiting some of the worst cases. It can be grim, but you'll get a panoramic view of Hawksbill Station in a hurry."

"I'd like to go."

Barrett gestured to Quesada and the three of them left

the building. This was a nightly ritual for Barrett, difficult as it was since he had hurt his foot. Before turning in, he visited the goofy ones and the psycho ones and the catatonic ones, tucked them in, wished them a good night and a healed mind in the morning. Someone had to show them that he cared. Barrett did.

Outside, Hahn peered up at the moon. It was nearly full tonight, shining like a burnished coin, its face a pale salmon color and hardly pockmarked at all.

"It looks so different here," Hahn said. "The craters—where are the craters?"

"Most of them haven't been formed yet," said Barrett. "A billion years is a long time even for the moon. Most of its upheavals are still ahead. We think it may still have an atmosphere, too. That's why it looks pink to us. Of course, Up Front hasn't bothered to send us much in the way of astronomical equipment. We can only guess."

Hahn started to say something. He cut himself off after one blurted syllable.

Quesada said, "Don't hold it back. What were you about to suggest?"

Hahn laughed in self-mockery. "That you ought to fly up there and take a look. It struck me as odd that you'd spend all these years here theorizing about whether the moon's got an atmosphere, and wouldn't ever once go up to look. But I forgot."

"It would be useful if we got a commute ship from Up Front," Barrett said. "But it hasn't occurred to them. All we can do is look. The moon's a popular place in '29, is it?"

"The biggest resort in the System," said Hahn. "I was there on my honeymoon. Leah and I—"

He stopped again.

Barrett said hurriedly, "This is Bruce Valdosto's hut. He cracked up a few weeks ago. When we go in, stand behind us so he doesn't see you. He might be violent with a stranger. He's unpredictable."

Valdosto was a husky man in his late forties, with

swarthy skin, coarse curling black hair, and the broadest shoulders any man had ever had. Sitting down, he looked even burlier than Jim Barrett, which was saying a great deal. But Valdosto had short, stumpy legs, the legs of a man of ordinary stature tacked to the trunk of a giant, which spoiled the effect completely. In his years Up Front he had totally refused any prosthesis. He believed in living with deformities.

Right now he was strapped into a webfoam cradle. His domed forehead was flecked with beads of sweat, his eyes were glittering beadily in the darkness. He was a very sick man. Once he had been clear-minded enough to throw a sleet-bomb into a meeting of the Council of Syndics, giving a dozen of them a bad case of gamma poisoning, but now he scarcely knew up from down, right from left.

Barrett leaned over him and said, "How are you, Bruce?"

"Who's that?"

"Jim. It's a beautiful night, Bruce. How'd you like to come outside and get some fresh air? The moon's almost full."

"I've got to rest. The committee meeting tomorrow—"

"It's been postponed."

"But how can it? The Revolution—"

"That's been postponed too. Indefinitely."

"Are they disbanding the cells?" Valdosto asked harshly.

"We don't know yet. We're waiting for orders. Come outside, Bruce. The air will do you good."

Muttering, Valdosto let himself be unlaced. Quesada and Barrett pulled him to his feet and propelled him through the door of the hut. Barrett caught sight of Hahn in the shadows, his face somber with shock.

They stood together outside the hut. Barrett pointed to the moon. "It's got such a lovely color here. Not like the dead thing Up Front. And look, look down there, Bruce.

The sea breaking on the rocky shore. Rudiger's out fishing. I can see his boat by moonlight."

"Striped bass," said Valdosto. "Sunnies. Maybe he'll catch some sunnies."

"There aren't any sunnies here. They haven't evolved yet." Barrett fished in his pocket and drew out something ridged and glossy, about two inches long. It was the exoskeleton of a small trilobite. He offered it to Valdosto, who shook his head.

"Don't give me that cockeyed crab."

"It's a trilobite, Bruce. It's extinct, but so are we. We're a billion years in our own past."

"You must be crazy," Valdosto said in a calm, low voice that belied his wild-eyed appearance. He took the trilobite from Barrett and hurled it against the rocks. "Cockeyed crab," he muttered.

Quesada shook his head sadly. He and Barrett led the sick man into the hut again. Valdosto did not protest as the medic gave him the sedative. His weary mind, rebelling entirely against the monstrous concept that he had been exiled to the inconceivably remote past, welcomed sleep.

When they went out Barrett saw Hahn holding the trilobite on his palm and staring at it in wonder. Hahn offered it to him, but Barrett brushed it away.

"Keep it if you like," he said. "There are more where I got that one."

They went on. They found Ned Altman beside his hut, crouching on his knees and patting his hands over the crude, lopsided form of what, from its exaggerated breasts and hips, appeared to be the image of a woman. He stood up when they appeared. Altman was a neat little man with yellow hair and nearly invisible white eyebrows. Unlike anyone else in the Station, he had actually been a government man once, fifteen years ago, before seeing through the myth of syndicalist capitalism and joining one of the underground factions. Eight years at Hawksbill Station had done things to him.

Altman pointed to his golem and said, "I hoped there'd

be lightning in the rain today. That'll do it, you know. But there isn't much lightning this time of year. She'll get up alive, and then I'll need you, Doc, to give her her shots and trim away some of the rough places."

Quesada forced a smile. "I'll be glad to do it, Ned. But you know the terms."

"Sure. When I'm through with her, you get her. You think I'm a goddamn monopolist? I'll share her. There'll be a waiting list. Just so you don't forget who made her, though. She'll remain mine, whenever I need her." He noticed Hahn. "Who are you?"

"He's new," Barrett said. "Lew Hahn. He came this afternoon."

"Ned Altman," said Altman with a courtly bow. "Formerly in government service. You're pretty young, aren't you? How's your sex orientation? Hetero?"

Hahn winced. "I'm afraid so."

"It's okay. I wouldn't touch you. I've got a project going, here. But I just want you to know, I'll put you on my list. You're young and you've probably got stronger needs than some of us. I won't forget about you, even though you're new here."

Quesada coughed. "You ought to get some rest now, Ned. Maybe there'll be lightning tomorrow."

Altman did not resist. The doctor took him inside and put him to bed, while Hahn and Barrett surveyed the man's handiwork. Hahn pointed toward the figure's middle.

"He's left out something essential," he said. "If he's planning to make love to this girl after he's finished creating her, he'd better—"

"It was there yesterday," said Barrett. "He must be changing orientation again." Quesada emerged from the hut. They went on, down the rocky path.

Barrett did not make the complete circuit that night. Ordinarily, he would have gone all the way down to Latimer's hut overlooking the sea, for Latimer was on his list of sick ones. But Barrett had visited Latimer once that day, and he didn't think his aching good leg was up to another hike that far. So after he and Quesada and Hahn had been to all of the easily accessible huts, and visited the man who prayed for alien beings to rescue him and the man who was trying to break into a parallel universe where everything was as it ought to be in the world and the man who lay on his cot sobbing for all his wakeful hours, Barrett said goodnight to his companions and allowed Quesada to escort Hahn back to his hut without him.

After observing Hahn for half a day, Barrett realized he did not know much more about him than when he had first dropped onto the Anvil. That was odd. But maybe Hahn would open up a little more, after he'd been here a while. Barrett stared up at the salmon moon, and reached into his pocket to finger the little trilobite before he remembered that he had given it to Hahn. He shuffled into his hut. He wondered how long ago Hahn had taken that lunar honeymoon trip.

Five

Rudiger's catch was spread out in front of the main building the next morning when Barrett came up for breakfast. He had had a good night's fishing, obviously. He usually did. Rudiger went out three or four nights a week, in the little dinghy that he had cobbled together a few years ago from salvaged materials, and he took with him a team of friends whom he had trained in the deft use of the trawling nets.

It was an irony that Rudiger, the anarchist, the man who believed in individualism and the abolition of all political institutions, should be so good at leading a team of fishermen. Rudiger didn't care for teamwork in the abstract. But it was hard to manipulate the nets alone, he had discovered. Hawksbill Station had many little ironies of that sort. Political theorists tend to swallow their theories when forced back on pragmatic measures of survival.

The prize of the catch was a cephalopod about a dozen feet long—a rigid conical tube out of which some limp squidlike tentacles dangled. Plenty of meat on that one, Barrett thought. Dozens of trilobites were arrayed around it, ranging in size from the inch-long kind to the three-footers with their baroquely involuted exoskeletons. Rudiger fished both for food and for science; evidently these trilobites were discards, species that he already had studied, or he wouldn't have left them here to go into the food hoppers. His hut was stacked ceiling-high with trilobites. It kept him sane to collect and analyze them, and no one begrudged him his hobby.

Near the heap of trilobites were some clusters of hinged brachiopods, looking like scallops that had gone awry, and a pile of snails. The warm, shallow waters just off the coastal shelf teemed with life, in striking contrast to the barren land. Rudiger had also brought in a mound of shiny black seaweed. Barrett hoped someone would gather all this stuff up and get it into their heat-sink cooler before it spoiled. The bacteria of decay worked a lot slower here than they did Up Front, but a few hours in the mild air would do Rudiger's haul no good.

Today Barrett planned to recruit some men for the annual Inland Sea expedition. Traditionally, he led that trek himself, but his injury made it impossible for him even to consider going any more. Each year, a dozen or so able-bodied men went out on a wide-ranging reconnaissance that took them in a big circle, looping northwestward until they reached the sea, then coming around to the south and back to the Station. One purpose of the trip was to gather any temporal garbage that might have materialized in the vicinity of the Station during the past year. There was no way of knowing how wide a margin of error had been allowed during the early attempts to set up the Station, and the scattershot technique of hurling material into the past had been pretty unreliable. New stuff was turning up all the time that had been aimed for Minus One Billion, Two Thousand Oh Five A.D., but which didn't get there until a few decades later. Hawksbill Station needed all the spare equipment it could get, and Barrett didn't miss a chance to round up any of the debris.

There was another reason for the Inland Sea expeditions, though. They served as a focus for the year, an annual ritual, something to peg a custom to. It was a rite of spring here. The dozen strongest men, going on foot to the distant rock-rimmed shores of the tepid sea that drowned the middle of North America, were performing the closest thing Hawksbill Station had to a religious function, although they did nothing more mystical when they reached the Inland Sea than to net a few trilobites and eat them. The trip meant more to Barrett himself than he had even suspected, also. He realized that now, when he was unable to go. He had led every such expedition for twenty years.

But last year he had gone scrabbling over boulders loosened by the tireless action of the waves, venturing into risky territory for no rational reason that he could name, and his aging muscles had betrayed him. Often at night he woke sweating to escape from the dream in which he relived that ugly moment: slipping and sliding, clawing at the rocks, a mass of stone dislodged from somewhere and crashing down with improbably agonizing impact on his foot, pinning him, crushing him. He could not forget the sound of grinding bones. Nor was he likely to lose the memory of the homeward march, across hundreds of miles of bare rock, his bulky body slung between the bowed forms of his companions. He thought he would lose the foot, but Quesada had spared him from the amputation. He simply could not touch the foot to the ground and put weight on it now, or ever again. It might have been simpler to have the dead appendage sliced off. Quesada vetoed that, though. "Who knows," he had said, "some day they might send us a transplant kit. I can't rebuild a leg that's been amputated." So Barrett had kept his crushed foot. But he had never been quite the same since, and now someone else would have to lead the march.

Who would it be, he asked himself?

Quesada was the likeliest. Next to Barrett, he was the strongest man here, in all the ways that it was important to be strong. But Quesada couldn't be spared at the Station. It might be handy to have a medic along on the trip, but it was vital to have one here. After some reflection Barrett put down Charley Norton as the leader. He added Ken Belardi—someone for Norton to talk to. Rudiger? A tower of strength last year after Barrett had been injured; Barrett didn't particularly want to let Rudiger leave the Station so long, though he needed able men for the expedition, true, but he didn't want to strip the home base down to invalids, crackpots, and psychotics. Rudiger stayed. Two of his fellow fishermen went on the list. So did Sid Hutchett and Arny Jean-Claude.

Barrett thought about putting Don Latimer in the group. Latimer was coming to be something of a borderline mental case, but he was rational enough except when he lapsed into his psionic meditations, and he'd pull his own weight on the expedition. On the other hand, Latimer was Lew Hahn's roommate, and Barrett wanted Latimer around to observe Hahn at close range. He toyed with the idea of sending both of them out, but nixed it. Hahn was still an unknown quantity. It was too risky to let him go with the Inland Sea party this year. Probably he'd be in next spring's group, though.

Finally Barrett had his dozen men chosen. He chalked their names on the slate in front of the mess hall, and found Charley Norton at breakfast to tell him he was in charge.

It felt strange to know that he'd have to stay home while the others went. It was an admission that he was beginning to abdicate after running this place so long. A crippled old man was what he was, whether he liked to admit it to himself or not, and that was something he'd have to come to terms with soon.

In the afternoon, the men of the Inland Sea expedition gathered to select their gear and plan their route. Barrett kept away from the meeting. This was Charley Norton's show, now. He'd made eight or ten trips, and he knew what to do. Barrett didn't want to interfere.

But some masochistic compulsion in him drove him to take a trek of his own. If he couldn't see the western waters this year, the least he could do was pay a visit to the Atlantic, in his own back yard. Barrett stopped off in the infirmary and, finding Quesada elsewhere, helped himself to a tube of neural depressant. He scrambled along the eastern trail until he was a few hundred yards from the main building, dropped his trousers, and quickly gave each thigh a jolt of the drug, first the good leg, then the gimpy one. That would numb the muscles just enough so that he'd be able to take an extended hike without feeling the fire of fatigue in his protesting joints. He'd pay for it, he knew, eight hours from now, when the depressant wore off and the full impact of his exertion hit him like a million daggers. But he was willing to accept that price.

The road to the sea was a long, lonely one. Hawksbill Station was perched on the eastern rim of Appalachia, more than eight hundred feet above sea level. During the first half dozen years, the men of the Station had reached the ocean by a suicidal route across sheer rock faces, but Barrett had incited a ten-year project to carve a path. Now wide steps descended to the Atlantic. Chopping them out of the rock had kept a lot of men busy for a long time, too busy to worry or to slip into insanity. Barrett regretted that he couldn't conceive some comparable works project to occupy them nowadays.

The steps formed a succession of shallow platforms that switchbacked to the edge of the water. Even for a healthy man it was a strenuous walk. For Barrett in his present condition it was an ordeal. It took him two hours to descend a distance that normally could be traversed in a quarter of that time. When he reached the bottom, he sank down exhaustedly on a flat rock licked by the waves, and dropped his crutch. The fingers of his left hand were cramped and gnarled from gripping the crutch, and his entire body was bathed in sweat.

The water looked gray and somehow oily. Barrett could not explain the prevailing colorlessness of the Late Cambrian world, with its somber sky and somber land and somber sea, but his heart quietly ached for a glimpse of green vegetation again. He missed chlorophyll. The dark wavelets lapped against his rock, pushing a mass of floating black seaweed back and forth. The sea stretched to infinity. He didn't have the faintest idea how much of Europe, if any, was above water in this epoch. At the best of times most of the planet was submerged; here, only a few hundred million years after the white-hot rocks of the land had pushed into view, it was likely that all that was above water on Earth was a strip of territory here and there. Had the Himalayas been born yet? The Rockies? The Andes? He knew the approximate outlines of Late Cambrian North America, but the rest was a mystery. Blanks in knowledge were not easy to fill when the only link with Up Front was by one-way transport; Hawksbill Station had to rely on the random assortment of reading matter that came back in time, and it was furiously frustrating to lack information that any college geology text could supply.

As he watched, a big trilobite unexpectedly came scuttering up out of the water. It was the spike-tailed kind, about a yard long, with an eggplant-purple shell and a bristling arrangement of slender spines along the margins. There seemed to be a lot of legs underneath. The trilobite crawled up on the shore—no sand, no beach, just a shelf of rock—and advanced until it was eight or ten feet from the waves.

Good for you, Barrett thought. Maybe you're the first one who ever came out on land to see what it was like. The pioneer. The trailblazer.

It occurred to him that this adventurous trilobite might well be the ancestor of all the land-dwelling creatures of the eons to come. It was biological nonsense, but Barrett's weary mind conjured a picture of an evolutionary procession, with fish and amphibians and reptiles and mammals and man all stemming in unbroken sequence from this grotesque armored thing that moved in uncertain circles near his feet.

And if I were to step on you, he thought?

A quick motion—the sound of crunching chitin—the wild scrabbling of a host of little legs—

And the whole chain of life snapped in its first link. Evolution undone. No land creatures ever developed. With the descent of that heavy foot all the future would change, and there would never have been any Hawksbill Station, no human race, no James Edward Barrett. In an instant he would have both revenge on those who had condemned him to live out his days in this place, and release from his sentence.

He did nothing. The trilobite completed its slow perambulation of the shoreline rocks and scuttered back into the sea unharmed.

The soft voice of Don Latimer said, "I saw you sitting down here, Jim. Do you mind if I join you?"

Barrett swung around, momentarily surprised. Latimer had come down from his hilltop hut so quietly that Barrett hadn't heard a thing. He recovered and grinned and beckoned Latimer to an adjoining rock.

"You fishing?" Latimer asked.

"Just sitting. An old man sunning himself."

"You took a hike like that just to sun yourself?" Latimer laughed. "Come off it. You're trying to get away from it all, and you probably wish I hadn't disturbed you."

"That's not so. Stay here. How's your new roommate getting along?"

"It's been strange," said Latimer. "That's one reason I came down here to talk to you." He leaned forward and peered searchingly into Barrett's eyes. "Jim, tell me: do you think I'm a madman?"

"Why should I?"

"The esping business. My attempt to break through to another realm of consciousness. I know you're tough-minded and skeptical. You probably think it's all a lot of nonsense."

Barrett shrugged and said, "If you want the blunt truth, I do. I don't have the remotest belief that you're going to get us anywhere, Don. I think it's a complete waste of time and energy for you to sit there for hours harnessing your psionic powers, or whatever it is you do. But no, I don't think you're crazy. I think you're entitled to your obsession and that you're going about a basically futile thing in a reasonably level-headed way. Fair enough?"

"More than fair. I don't ask you to put any credence in my research, but I don't want you to think I'm a total lunatic for trying it. It's important that you regard me as sane, or else what I want to tell you about Hahn won't be valid to you."

"I don't see the connection."

"It's this," said Latimer. "On the basis of one evening's acquaintance, I've formed an opinion about Hahn. It's the kind of an opinion that might be formed by a garden-variety paranoid, and if you think I'm nuts you're likely to discount my idea about Hahn."

"I don't think you're nuts. What's your idea?"

"That he's spying on us."

Barrett had to work hard to keep from emitting the guffaw that would shatter Latimer's fragile self-esteem. "Spying?" he said casually. "You can't mean that. How can anyone spy here? I mean, how can he report his findings?"

"I don't know," Latimer said. "But he asked me a million questions last night. About you, about Quesada, about some of the sick men. He wanted to know everything."

"The normal curiosity of a new man."

"Jim, he was taking notes. I saw him after he thought I was asleep. He sat up for two hours writing it all down in a little book."

Barrett frowned. "Maybe he's going to write a novel about us."

"I'm serious," Latimer said. "Questions—notes. And he's shifty. Try to get him to talk about himself!"

"I did. I didn't learn much."

"Do you know why he's been sent here?"

"No."

"Neither do I," said Latimer. "Political crimes, he said, but he was vague as hell. He hardly seemed to know what the present government was up to, let alone what his own opinions were toward it. I don't detect any passionate philosophical convictions in Mr. Hahn. And you know as well as I do that Hawksbill Station is the refuse heap for revolutionaries and agitators and subversives and all sorts of similar trash, but that we've never had any other kind of prisoner here."

Barrett said coolly, "I agree that Hahn's a puzzle. But who could he be spying for? He's got no way to file a report, if he's a government agent. He's stranded here for keeps, same as the rest of us."

"Maybe he was sent to keep an eye on us—to make sure we aren't cooking up some way to escape. Maybe he's a volunteer who willingly gave up his twenty-first century life so he could come among us and thwart anything we might be hatching. Perhaps they're afraid we've invented forward time travel. Or that we've become a threat to the sequence of the time-lines. Anything. So Hahn comes among us to snoop around and block any dangers before they arrive."

Barrett felt a twinge of alarm. He saw how close to paranoia Latimer was hewing, now: in half a dozen sentences he had journeyed from the rational expression of some justifiable suspicions to the fretful fear that the men from Up Front were going to take steps to choke off the escape route that he was so close to perfecting.

He kept his voice level as he told Latimer, "I don't think you need to worry, Don. Hahn's an odd one, but he's not here to make trouble for us. The fellows Up Front have already made all the trouble for us they ever will."

"Would you keep an eye on him, anyway?"

"You know I will. And don't hesitate to let me know if Hahn does anything else out of the ordinary. You're in a better spot to notice than anyone else."

"I'll be watching," Latimer said. "We can't tolerate any spies from Up Front among us." He got to his feet and gave Barrett a pleasant smile. "I'll let you get back to your sunning now, Jim."

Latimer went up the path. Barrett eyed him until he was close to the top, only a faint dot against the stony backdrop. After a long while Barrett seized his crutch and levered himself to his feet. He stood staring down at the surf, dipping the tip of his crutch into the water to send a couple of little crawling things scurrying away. At length he turned and began the long, slow climb back to the Station.

Six

A couple of days passed before Barrett had the chance to draw Lew Hahn aside for a spot of political discussion. The Inland Sea party had set out, and in a way that was too bad, for Barrett could have used Charley Norton's services in penetrating Hahn's armor. Norton was the most gifted theorist around, a man who could weave a tissue of dialectic from the least promising material. If anyone could find out the depth of Hahn's Marxist commitment, if any, it was Norton. But Norton was leading the expedition, so Barrett had to do the interrogating himself. His Marxism was a trifle rusty, and he couldn't thread his path through the Leninist, Stalinist, Trotskyite, Khrushchevist, Maoist, Berenkovskyite and Mgumbweist schools with Charley Norton's skills. Yet he knew what questions to ask.

He picked a rainy evening when Hahn seemed to be in a fairly outgoing mood. There had been an hour's entertainment that night, an ingenious computer-composed film that Sid Hutchett had programmed last week. Up Front had been kind enough to ship back a modest computer, and Hutchett had rigged it to do animations by specifying line widths and lengths, shades of gray, and progression of raster units. It was a simple but remarkably clever business, and it brightened a dull night.

Afterward, sensing that Hahn was relaxed enough to lower his guard a bit, Barrett said, "Hutchett's a rare one. Did you meet him before he went on the trip?"

"Tall fellow with a sharp nose and no chin?"

"That's the one. A clever boy. He was the top computer man for the Continental Liberation Front until they caught him in '19. He programmed that fake broadcast in which Chancellor Dantell denounced his own regime. Remember?"

"I'm not sure I do." Hahn frowned. "How long ago was this?"

"The broadcast was in 2018. Would that be before your time? Only eleven years ago—"

"I was nineteen then," said Hahn. "I guess I wasn't very politically sophisticated."

"Too busy studying economics, I guess."

Hahn grinned. "That's right. Deep in the dismal science."

"And you never heard that broadcast? Or even heard *of* it?"

"I must have forgotten."

"The biggest hoax of the century," Barrett said, "and you forgot it. You know the Continental Liberation Front, of course."

"Of course." Hahn looked uneasy.

"Which group did you say you were with?"

"The People's Crusade for Liberty."

"I don't know it. One of the newer groups?"

"Less than five years old. It started in California."

"What's its program?"

"Oh, the usual," Hahn said. "Free elections, representative government, an opening of the security files, restoration of civil liberties."

"And the economic orientation? Pure Marxist or one of the offshoots?"

"Not really any, I guess. We believed in a kind of—well, capitalism with some goverment restraints."

"A little to the right of state socialism, and a little to the left of laissez faire?" Barrett suggested.

"Something like that."

"But that system was tried and failed, wasn't it? It had its day. It led inevitably to total socialism, which produced the compensating backlash of syndicalist capitalism, and then we got a government that pretended to be libertarian while actually stifling all individual liberties in the name of freedom. So if your group simply wanted to turn the clock back to 1955, say, there couldn't be much to its ideas."

Hahn looked bored. "You've got to understand I wasn't in the top ideological councils."

"Just an economist?"

"That's it. I drew up plans for the conversion to our system."

"Basing your work on the modified liberalism of Ricardo?"

"Well, in a sense."

"And avoiding the tendency to fascism that was found in the thinking of Keynes?"

"You could say so," Hahn said. He stood up, flashing a quick, vague smile. "Look, Jim, I'd love to argue this further with you some other time, but I've really got to go now. Ned Altman talked me into coming around and helping him do a lightning-dance to bring that pile of dirt to life. So if you don't mind—"

Hahn beat a hasty retreat.

Barrett was more perplexed than ever, now. Hahn hadn't been "arguing" anything. He had been carrying on a lame and feeble conversation, letting himself be pushed hither and thither by Barrett's questions. And he had spouted a lot of nonsense. He didn't seem to know Keynes from Ricardo, nor to care about it, which was odd for a self-professed economist. He didn't have a shred of an idea what his own political party stood for. He had so little revolutionary background that he was unaware even of Hutchett's astonishing hoax of eleven years back.

He seemed phony from top to bottom.

How was it possible that this kid had been deemed worthy of exile to Hawksbill Station, anyhow? Only the top firebrands went there. Sentencing a man to Hawksbill was like sentencing him to death, and it wasn't done lightly. Barrett couldn't imagine why Hahn was here. He seemed genuinely distressed at being exiled, and evidently he had left a beloved young wife behind, but nothing else rang true about the man.

Was he—as Latimer suggested—some kind of spy?

Barrett rejected the idea out of hand. He didn't want Latimer's paranoia infecting him. The government wasn't likely to send anyone on a one-way trip to the Late Cambrian just to spy on a bunch of aging revolutionaries who could never make trouble again. But what *was* Hahn doing here, then?

He would bear further watching, Barrett thought.

Barrett took care of some of the watching himself. But he had plenty of assistance. Latimer. Altman. Six or seven others. Latimer had recruited most of the ambulatory psycho cases, the ones who were superficially functional but full of all kinds of fears and credulities.

They were keeping an eye on the new man.

On the fifth day after his arrival, Hahn went out fishing in Rudiger's crew. Barrett stood for a long time on the edge of the world, watching the little boat bobbing in the surging Atlantic. Rudiger never went far from shore—eight hundred, a thousand yards out—but the water was rough even there. The waves came rolling in with X thousand miles of gathered impact behind them. A continental shelf sloped off at a wide angle, so that even at a substantial distance off shore the water wasn't very deep. Rudiger had taken soundings up to a mile out, and had reported depths no greater than 160 feet. Nobody had gone past a mile.

It wasn't that they were afraid of falling off the side of the world if they went too far east. It was simply that a mile was a long distance to row in an open boat, using stubby oars made from old packing cases. Up Front hadn't thought to spare an outboard motor for them.

Looking toward the horizon, Barrett had an odd thought. He had been told that the women's equivalent of Hawksbill Station was safely segregated out of reach, a couple of hundred million years up the time-line. But how did he know that? There could be another Station somewhere else in this very year, and they'd never know about it. A camp of women, say, living on the far side of the ocean, or even across the Inland Sea.

It wasn't very likely, he knew. With the entire past to pick from, the edgy men Up Front wouldn't take any chance that the two groups of exiles might get together and spawn a tribe of little subversives. They'd take every precaution to put an impenetrable barrier of epochs between them. Yet Barrett thought he could make it sound convincing to the other men. With a little effort he could get them to believe in the existence of several simultaneous Hawksbill Stations scattered on this level of time.

Which could be our salvation, he thought.

The instances of degenerative psychosis were beginning to snowball, now. Too many men had been here too long, and one crackup was starting to feed the next, in this blank lifeless world where humans were never meant to live. The men needed projects to keep them going. They were starting to slip off into harebrained projects, like Altman's Frankenstein girlfriend and Latimer's psi pursuit.

Suppose, Barrett thought, I could get them steamed up about reaching the other continents?

A round-the-world expedition. Maybe they could build some kind of big ship. That would keep a lot of men busy for a long time. And they'd need navigational equipment —compasses, sextants, chronometers, whatnot. Somebody would have to design an improvised radio, too. It was the kind of project that might take thirty or forty years. A focus for our energies, Barrett thought. Of course, I won't live to see the ship set sail. But even so, it's a way of staving off collapse. We've built our staircase to the sea. Now we need something bigger to do. Idle hands make for idle minds. . . . sick minds. . . .

He liked the idea he had hatched. For several weeks, now, Barrett had been worrying about the deteriorating state of affairs in the Station, and looking for some way to cope with it. Now he thought he had his way.

Turning, he saw Latimer and Altman standing behind him.

"How long have you been there?" he asked.

"Two minutes," said Latimer. "We brought you something to look at."

Altman nodded vigorously. "You ought to read it. We brought it for you to read."

"What is it?"

Latimer handed over a folded sheaf of papers. "I found this tucked away in Hahn's bunk after he went out with Rudiger. I know I'm not supposed to be invading his privacy, but I had to have a look at what he's been writing. There it is. He's a spy, all right."

Barrett glanced at the papers in his hand. "I'll read it a little later. What is it about?"

"It's a description of the Station, and a profile of most of the men in it," said Latimer. He smiled frostily. "Hahn's private opinion of me is that I've gone mad. His private opinion of you is a little more flattering, but not much."

Altman said, "He's also been hanging around the Hammer."

"*What?*"

"I saw him going there late last night. He went into the building. I followed him. He was looking at the Hammer."

"Why didn't you tell me that right away?" Barrett snapped.

"I wasn't sure it was important," Altman said. "I had to talk it over with Don first. And I couldn't do that until Hahn had gone out fishing."

Sweat burst out on Barrett's face. "Listen, Ned, if you ever catch Hahn going near the time-travel equipment again, you let me know in a hurry. Without consulting Don or anyone else. Clear?"

"Clear," said Altman. He giggled. "You know what I think? They've decided to exterminate us Up Front. Hahn's been sent here to check us out as a suicide volunteer. Then they're going to send a bomb through the Hammer and blow the Station up. We ought to wreck the Hammer and Anvil before they get a chance."

"But why would they send a suicide volunteer?" Latimer asked. "Unless they've got some way to rescue their spy—"

"In any case we shouldn't take any chance," Altman argued. "Wreck the Hammer. Make it impossible for them to bomb us from Up Front."

"That might be a good idea. But—"

"Shut up, both of you," Barrett growled. "Let me look at these papers."

He walked a few steps away from them and sat down on a shelf of rock. He unfolded the sheaf. He began to read.

Seven

Hahn had a cramped, crabbed handwriting that packed a maximum of information into a minimum of space, as though he regarded it as a mortal sin to waste paper. Fair enough; paper was a scarce commodity here, and evidently Hahn had brought these sheets with him from Up Front. His script was clear, though. So were his opinions. Painfully so.

He had written an analysis of conditions at Hawksbill Station, setting forth in about five thousand words everything that Barrett knew was going sour here. He had neatly ticked off the men as aging revolutionaries in whom the old fervor had turned rancid; he listed the ones who were certifiably psycho, and the ones who were on the edge, and the ones who were hanging on, like Quesada and Norton and Rudiger. Barrett was interested to see that Hahn rated even those three as suffering from severe strain and likely to fly apart at any moment. To him, Quesada and Norton and Rudiger seemed just about as stable as when they had first dropped onto the Anvil of Hawksbill Station; but that was possibly the distorting effect of his own blurred perceptions. To an outsider like Hahn, the view was different and perhaps more accurate.

Barrett forced himself not to skip ahead to Hahn's evaluation of him.

He wasn't pleased when he came to it. "Barrett," Hahn had written, "is like a mighty beam that's been gnawed from within by termites. He looks solid, but one good push would break him apart. A recent injury to his foot has evidently had a bad effect on him. The other men say he used to be physically vigorous and derived much of his authority from his size and strength. Now he can hardly walk. But I feel the trouble with Barrett is inherent in the life of Hawksbill Station, and doesn't have much to do with his lameness. He's been cut off from normal human drives for too long. The exercise of power here has provided the illusion of stability for him, but it's power in a vacuum, and things have happened within Barrett of which he's totally unaware. He's in bad need of therapy. He may be beyond help."

Barrett read that several times. *Gnawed from within*

*by termites. . . . one good push. . . . things have happened
within him. . . . bad need of therapy. . . . beyond help. . . .*

He was less angered than he thought he should have
been. Hahn was entitled to his views. Barrett finally
stopped rereading his profile and pushed his way to the
last page of Hahn's essay. It ended with the words,
"Therefore I recommend prompt termination of the
Hawksbill Station penal colony and, where possible, the
therapeutic rehabilitation of its inmates."

What the hell was this?

It sounded like the report of a parole commissioner!
But there was no parole from Hawksbill Station. That
final sentence let all the viability of what had gone before
bleed away. Hahn was pretending to be composing a report to the government Up Front, obviously. But a wall
two billion years thick made filing of that report impossible. So Hahn was suffering from delusions, just like
Altman and Valdosto and the others. In his fevered mind
he believed he could send messages Up Front, pompous
documents delineating the flaws and foibles of his fellow
prisoners.

That raised a chilling prospect. Hahn might be crazy,
but he hadn't been in the Station long enough to have
gone crazy here. He must have brought his insanity with
him.

What if they had stopped using Hawksbill Station as a
camp for political prisoners, Barrett asked himself, and
were starting to use it as an insane asylum?

A cascade of psychos descending on them. Men who
had gone honorably buggy under the stress of confinement
would have to make room for ordinary bedlamites. Barrett shivered. He folded up Hahn's papers and handed
them to Latimer, who was sitting a few yards away, watching him intently.

"What did you think of that?" Latimer asked.

"I think it's hard to evaluate. But possibly friend Hahn
is emotionally disturbed. Put this stuff back exactly where

you got it, Don. And don't give Hahn the faintest inkling that you've read or removed it."

"Right."

"And come to me whenever you think there's something I ought to know about him," Barrett said. "He may be a very sick boy. He may need all the help we can give."

The fishing expedition returned in early afternoon. Barrett saw that the dinghy was overflowing with the haul, and Hahn, coming into the camp with his arms full of gaffed trilobites, looked sunburned and pleased with his outing. Barrett came over to inspect the catch. Rudiger was in an effusive mood, and held up a bright-red crustacean that might have been the great-great-grandfather of all boiled lobsters, except that it had no front claws and a wicked-looking triple spike where a tail should have been. It was about two feet long, and ugly.

"A new species!" Rudiger crowed. "There's nothing like this in any museum. I wish I could put it where it would be found. Some mountaintop, maybe."

"If it could be found, it *would* have been found," Barrett reminded him. "Some paleontologist of the twentieth century would have dug it out. So forget it, Mel."

Hahn said, "I've been wondering about that point. How is it nobody Up Front ever dug up the fossil remains of Hawksbill Station? Aren't they worried that one of the early fossil hunters will find it in the Cambrian strata and raise a fuss?"

Barrett shook his head. "For one thing, no paleontologist from the beginning of the science to the founding of the Station in 2005 ever *did* dig up Hawksbill. That's a matter of record, so there was nothing to worry about. If it came to light after 2005, why, everyone would know what it was. No paradox there."

"Besides," said Rudiger sadly, "in another billion years this whole strip of rock will be on the floor of the Atlantic, with a couple of miles of sediment over it. There's not a chance we'll be found. Or that anyone Up Front will ever see this guy I caught today. Not that I give a damn. I've seen him. I'll dissect him. Their loss."

"But you regret the fact that science will never know of this species," Hahn said.

"Sure I do. But is it my fault? Science does know of this species. Me. I'm science. I'm the leading paleontologist of this epoch. Can I help it if I can't publish my discoveries in the professional journals?" He scowled and walked away, carrying the big red crustacean.

Hahn and Barrett looked at each other. They smiled, in a natural mutual response to Rudiger's grumbled outburst. Then Barrett's smile faded.

termites. . . . one good push. . . . therapy. . . .

"Something wrong?" Hahn asked.

"Why?"

"You looked so bleak, all of a sudden."

"My foot gave me a twinge," Barrett said. "It does that, you know. Here. I'll give you a hand carrying those things. We'll have fresh trilobite cocktail tonight."

Eight

A little before midnight, Barrett was awakened by footsteps outside his hut. As he sat up, groping for the luminescence switch, Ned Altman came blundering through the door. Barrett blinked at him.

"What's the matter?"

"Hahn!" Altman rasped. "He's fooling around with the Hammer again. We just saw him go into the building."

Barrett shed his sleepiness like a seal bursting out of water. Ignoring the insistent throb in his left leg, he pulled himself from his bed and grabbed some clothing. He was more apprehensive than he wanted Altman to see. If Hahn, fooling around with the temporal mechanism, accidentally smashed the Hammer, they might never get replacement equipment from Up Front. Which would mean that all future shipments of supplies—if there were any—would come as random shoots that might land in any old year. What business did Hahn have with the machine, anyway?

Altman said, "Latimer's up there keeping an eye on him. He got suspicious when Hahn didn't come back to the hut, and he got me, and we went looking for him. And there he was, sniffing around the Hammer."

"Doing what?"

"I don't know. As soon as we saw him go in, I came down here to get you. Don's watching."

Barrett stumped his way out of the hut and did his best to run toward the main building. Pain shot like trails of hot acid up the lower half of his body. The crutch dug mercilessly into his left armpit as he leaned all his weight into it. His crippled foot, swinging freely, burned with a cold glow. His right leg, which was carrying most of the burden, creaked and popped. Altman ran breathlessly alongside him. The Station was terribly silent at this hour.

As they passed Quesada's hut, Barrett considered waking the medic and taking him along. He decided against it. Whatever trouble Hahn might be up to, Barrett felt he could handle it himself. There was some strength left in the old gnawed beam, after all.

Latimer stood at the entrance to the main dome. He was right at the edge of panic, or perhaps over the edge. He seemed to be gibbering with fear and shock. Barrett had never seen a man gibber before.

He clamped a big paw on Latimer's thin shoulder and said harshly, "Where is he? Where's Hahn?"

"He—disappeared."

"What do you mean? Where did he go?"

Latimer moaned. His face was fish-belly white. "He got onto the Anvil," Latimer blurted. "The light came on —the glow. And then Hahn disappeared!"

"No," Barrett said. "It isn't possible. You must be mistaken."

"I saw him go!"

"He's hiding somewhere in the building," Barrett insisted. "Close that door! Search for him!"

Altman said, "He probably did disappear, Jim. If Don says he disappeared—"

"He climbed right on the Anvil. Then everything turned red and he was gone."

Barrett clenched his fists. There was a white-hot blaze just behind his forehead that almost made him forget about his foot. He saw his mistake, now. He had depended for his espionage on two men who were patently and unmistakably insane, and that had been itself a not very sane thing to do. A man is known by his choice of lieutenants. Well, he had relied on Altman and Latimer, and now they were giving him the sort of information that such spies could be counted on to supply.

"You're hallucinating," he told Latimer curtly. "Ned, go wake Quesada and get him here right away. You, Don, you stand here by the entrance, and if Hahn shows up I want you to scream at the top of your lungs. I'm going to search the building for him."

"Wait," Latimer said. He seemed to be in control of himself again. "Jim, do you remember when I asked you if you thought I was crazy? You said you didn't. You trusted me. Well, don't stop trusting me now. I tell you I'm not hallucinating. I saw Hahn disappear. I can't explain it, but I'm rational enough to know what I saw."

In a milder tone Barrett said, "All right. Maybe so. Stay by the door, anyway. I'll run a quick check."

He started to make the circuit of the dome, beginning with the room where the Hammer was located. Everything seemed to be in order there. No Hawksbill Field glow was in evidence, and nothing had been disturbed. The room had no closets or cupboards in which Hahn could be hiding. When he had inspected it thoroughly, Barrett moved on, looking into the infirmary, the mess hall, the kitchen, the recreation room. He looked high and low. No Hahn. Of course, there were plenty of places in those rooms where Hahn might have secreted himself, but Barrett doubted that he was there. So it had all been some feverish fantasy of Latimer's, then. He completed the route and found himself back at the main entrance. Latimer still stood guard there. He had been joined by a sleepy Quesada. Altman, pale and shaky-looking, was just outside the door.

"What's happening?" Quesada asked.

"I'm not sure," said Barrett. "Don and Ned had the idea they saw Lew Hahn fooling around with the time equipment. I've checked the building, and he's not here, so maybe they made a little mistake. I suggest you take them both into the infirmary and give them a shot of something to settle their nerves, and we'll all try to get back to sleep."

Latimer said, "I tell you, I saw—"

"Shut up!" Altman broke in. "Listen! What's that noise?"

Barrett listened. The sound was clear and loud: the hissing whine of ionization. It was the sound produced by a functioning Hawksbill Field. Suddenly there were goose-pimples on his flesh. In a low voice he said, "The field's on. We're probably getting some supplies."

"At this hour?" said Latimer.

"We don't know what time it is Up Front. All of you stay here. I'll check the Hammer."

"Perhaps I ought to go with you," Quesada suggested mildly.

"Stay here!" Barrett thundered. He paused, embarrassed at his own explosive show of wrath. "It only takes one of us. I'll be right back."

Without waiting for further dissent, he pivoted and limped down the hall to the Hammer room. He shouldered the door open and looked in. There was no need for him to switch on the light. The red glow of the Hawksbill Field illuminated everything.

Barrett stationed himself just within the door. Hardly daring to breathe, he stared fixedly at the Hammer, watching as the glow deepened through various shades of pink toward crimson, and then spread until it enfolded the waiting Anvil beneath it. An endless moment passed.

Then came the implosive thunderclap, and Lew Hahn dropped out of nowhere and lay for a moment in temporal shock on the broad plate of the Anvil.

Nine

In the darkness, Hahn did not notice Barrett at first. He sat up slowly, shaking off the stunning effects of a trip through time. After a few seconds he pushed himself toward the lip of the Anvil and let his legs dangle over it. He swung them to get the circulation going. He took a series of deep breaths. Finally he slipped to the floor. The glow of the field had gone out in the moment of his arrival, and so he moved warily, as though not wanting to bump into anything.

Abruptly Barrett switched on the light and said, "What have you been up to, Hahn?"

The younger man recoiled as though he had been jabbed in the gut. He gasped, hopped backward a few steps, and flung up both hands in a defensive gesture.

"Answer me," Barrett said.

Hahn regained his equilibrium. He shot a quick glance past Barrett's bulky form toward the hallway and said, "Let me go, will you? I can't explain now."

"You'd better explain now."

"It'll be easier for everyone if I don't," said Hahn. "Please. Let me pass."

Barrett continued to block the door. "I want to know where you've been. What have you been doing with the Hammer."

"Nothing. Just studying it."

"You weren't in this room a minute ago. Then you appeared. Where'd you come from, Hahn?"

"You're mistaken. I was standing right behind the Hammer. I didn't—"

"I saw you drop down on the Anvil. You took a time trip, didn't you?"

"No."

"Don't lie to me! You've got some way of going forward in time, isn't that so? You've been spying on us, and you just went somewhere to file your report—somewhere—and now you're back."

Hahn's forehead was glistening. He said, "I warn you, don't ask too many questions. You'll know everything in due time. This isn't the time. Please, now. Let me pass."

"I want answers first," Barrett said. He realized that he was trembling. He already knew the answers, and they were answers that shook him to the core of his soul. He knew where Hahn had been.

But Hahn had to admit it himself.

Hahn said nothing. He took a couple of hesitant steps toward Barrett, who did not move. He seemed to be gathering momentum for a rush at the doorway.

Barrett said, "You aren't getting out of here until you tell me what I want to know."

Hahn charged.

Barrett planted himself squarely, crutch braced against the doorframe, his good leg flat on the floor, and waited for the younger man to reach him. He figured he outweighed Hahn by eighty pounds. That might be enough to balance the fact that he was spotting Hahn thirty years and one leg. They came together, and Barrett drove his hands down onto Hahn's shoulders, trying to hold him, to force him back into the room.

Hahn gave an inch or two. He looked up at Barrett without speaking and pushed forward again.

"Don't—don't—" Barrett grunted. "I won't let you—"

"I don't want to do this," Hahn said.

He pushed again. Barrett felt himself bucking under the impact. He dug his hands as hard as he could into Hahn's shoulders, and tried to shove the other man backward into the room, but Hahn held firm and all of Barrett's energy was converted into a backward thrust rebounding on himself. He lost control of his crutch, and it slithered out from under his arm. For one agonizing moment Barrett's full weight rested on the crushed uselessness of his left foot, and then, as though his limbs were melting away beneath him, he began to sink toward the floor. He landed with a reverberating crash.

Quesada, Altman, and Latimer came rushing in. Barrett writhed in pain on the floor. Hahn stood over him, looking unhappy, his hands locked together.

"I'm sorry," he said. "You shouldn't have tried to muscle me like that."

Barrett glowered at him. "You were traveling in time, weren't you? You can answer me now!"

"Yes," Hahn said at last. "I went Up Front."

An hour later, after Quesada had pumped him with enough neural depressants to keep him from jumping out of his skin, Barrett got the full story. Hahn hadn't wanted to reveal it so soon, but he had changed his mind after his little scuffle.

It was all very simple. Time travel now worked in both directions. The glib, impressive noises about the flow of entropy had turned out to be just noises.

"How long has this been known?" Barrett asked.

"At least five years. We aren't sure yet exactly when the breakthrough came. After we're finished going through all the suppressed records of the former government—"

"The former government?"

Hahn nodded. "The revolution came in January. Not really a violent one, either. The syndicalists just mildewed from within, and when they got the first push they fell over."

"Was it mildew?" Barrett asked, coloring. "Or termites? Keep your metaphors straight."

Hahn glanced away. "Anyway, the government fell. We've got a provisional liberal regime in office now. Don't ask me much about it. I'm not a political theorist. I'm not even an economist. You guessed as much."

"What are you, then?"

"A policeman," Hahn said. "Part of the commission that's investigating the prison system of the former government. Including this prison."

Barrett looked at Quesada, then at Hahn. Thoughts were streaming turbulently through him, and he could not remember when he had last been so overwhelmed by events. He had to work hard to keep from breaking into the shakes again. His voice quavered a little as he said, "You came back to observe Hawksbill Station, right? And you went Up Front tonight to tell them what you saw here. You think we're a pretty sad bunch, eh?"

"You've all been under heavy stress here," Hahn said. "Considering the circumstances of your imprisonment—"

Quesada broke in. "If there's a liberal government in power, now, and it's possible to travel both ways in time, then am I right in assuming that the Hawksbill prisoners are going to be sent Up Front?"

"Of course," said Hahn. "It'll be done as soon as possible. That's been the whole purpose of my reconnaissance mission. To find out if you people were still alive, first, and then to see what shape you're in, how badly in need of treatment you are. You'll be given every available benefit of modern therapy, naturally. No expense spared to—"

Barrett scarcely paid attention to Hahn's words. He had been fearing something like this all night, ever since Altman had told him Hahn was monkeying with the Hammer, but he had never fully allowed himself to believe that it could really be possible.

He saw his kingdom crumbling, now.

He saw himself returned to a world he could not begin to comprehend—a lame Rip van Winkle, coming back after twenty years.

He saw himself leaving a place that had become his home.

Barrett said tiredly, "You know, some of the men aren't going to be able to adapt to the shock of freedom. It might just kill them to be dumped into the real world again. I mean the advanced psychos—Valdosto, and such."

"Yes," Hahn said. "I've mentioned them in my report."

"It'll be necessary to get them ready for a return in gradual stages. It might take several years to condition them to the idea. It might even take longer than that."

"I'm no therapist," said Hahn. "Whatever the doctors think is right for them is what'll be done. Maybe it will be necessary to keep them here. I can see where it would be pretty potent to send them back, after they've spent all these years believing there's no return."

"More than that," said Barrett. "There's a lot of work that can be done here. Scientific work. Exploration. I don't think Hawksbill Station ought to be closed down."

"No one said it would be. We have every intention of keeping it going. But not as a prison. The prison concept is out."

"Good," Barrett said. He fumbled for his crutch, found it, and got heavily to his feet. Quesada moved toward him as though to steady him, but Barrett shook him off. "Let's go outside," he said.

They left the building. A gray mist had come in over the Station, and a fine drizzle had begun to fall. Barrett looked around at the scattering of huts. At the ocean, dimly visible to the east in the faint moonlight. He thought of Charley Norton and the party that had gone on the annual expedition to the Inland Sea. That bunch was going to be in for a real surprise, when they got back here in a few weeks and discovered that everybody was free to go home.

Very strangely, Barrett felt a sudden pressure forming around his eyelids, as of tears trying to force their way out into the open.

Then he turned to Hahn and Quesada. In a low voice

he said, "Have you followed what I've been trying to tell you? Someone's got to stay here and ease the transition for the sick men who won't be able to stand the shock of return. Someone's got to keep the base running. Someone's got to explain things to the new men who'll be coming back here, the scientists."

"Naturally," Hahn said.

"The one who does that—the one who stays behind—I think it ought to be someone who knows the Station well, someone who's fit to return Up Front, but who's willing to make the sacrifice and stay. Do you follow me? A volunteer." They were smiling at him now. Barrett wondered if there might not be something patronizing about those smiles. He wondered if he might not be a little too transparent. To hell with both of them, he thought. He sucked the Cambrian air into his lungs until his chest swelled grandly.

"I'm offering to stay," Barrett said in a loud tone. He glared at them to keep them from objecting. But they wouldn't dare object, he knew. In Hawksbill Station, he was the king. And he meant to keep it that way. "I'll be the volunteer," he said. "I'll be the one who stays."

He looked out over his kingdom from the top of the hill.

ROBERT SILVERBERG was born and educated in New York City, and lives there now with his wife, Barbara. He is the author of many science fiction novels, including *The Masks of Time, To Live Again, Thorns, Hawksbill Station, Up the Line*, and others, as well as numerous short stories. He has won two Hugo Awards and one Nebula, and is a Past-President of the Science Fiction Writers of America.

Mr. Silverberg has also written a number of nonfiction books on historical and archaeological subjects, including *Mound Builders of Ancient America, The Challenge of Climate*, and *Lost Cities and Vanished Civilizations*.

He was American Guest of Honor at the 1970 World Science Fiction Convention at Heidelberg, Germany.

THE TAR-AIYM KRANG

by

Alan Dean Foster

The Planet Moth . . .

so named because of its beautiful "wings"—great
golden clouds forever suspended in space.

And like its namesake, the planet attracted unwary
travelers—a teeming, constantly shifting horde
that provided a comfortable income for certain
quick-witted fellows like Flinx, who was experienced in extra-legal and nefarious means of ac-
complishing his ends. Yet not even Flinx held the
real key to the ultimate power of the Krang—an
artifact older than time and still functioning . . .

95¢

THE GOREAN CYCLE—COUNTER-EART

John Norman

TARNSMAN OF GOR	95¢
OUTLAW OF GOR	95¢
PRIEST-KINGS OF GOR	95¢
NOMADS OF GOR	95¢
ASSASSIN OF GOR	95¢
RAIDERS OF GOR	95¢

Here is the magnificent world of Gor, known also as Counter-Earth, a planet as strangely populated, as threatening, as beautiful as any you are likely to encounter in the great works of fiction. Here too is Tarl Cabot—the one picked out of millions to be trained and schooled and disciplined by the best teachers, swordsmen, bowmen on Gor . . . Toward what end, what mission, what purpose?

Only Gor holds the answer.